"*The River* is a captivating story told by a masterful storyteller. Page by page, the characters drew me in and  o. *The River* awakened the advent ought provoking, challenging, and *River* and not be impacted . . . I cel

JORDAN RUBIN
NEW YORK TIMES BESTSELLING AUTHOR,
THE MAKER'S DIET

"*The River* is a beautifully crafted novel by a gifted communicator. Michael Neale has successfully parlayed his ability to inspire from the performing platform to the written page. The story of *The River* will inspire its readers to live a life they were destined for!"

JOHN C. MAXWELL
FOUNDER OF EQUIP
AND THE JOHN MAXWELL COMPANY

"*The River* is a work of art. Michael Neale is a gifted writer. I was enthralled with every page. It gripped me and I could not put it down!"

LOWELL "BUD" PAXSON
FOUNDER
ION TELEVISION NETWORK

"Truly riveting. I felt like I was living the story and experiencing the events as they unfolded and couldn't put the book down. Michael Neale has woven wonder and wisdom into a story that will continue to inspire hearts for years to come. Read this book, it will open your eyes."

PAUL BALOCHE
AWARD-WINNING SONGWRITER, RECORDING ARTIST

"I've heard Michael Neale tell stories for years. I've been encouraged, uplifted, made to laugh, and brought to tears by them. *The River* does this and so much more. This story got a hold of me and wouldn't let go. I believe this novel will inspire many to conquer their fears, and really live!

DR. J. TODD MULLINS
LEAD PASTOR
CHRIST FELLOWSHIP CHURCH
PALM BEACH GARDENS, FLORIDA

"The story of *The River* is inspiring and uplifting! Reaching deep into your heart from the opening pages, *The River* and its cast of characters takes you on a life-changing journey. Everyone needs to read it. I believe this story will impact the world!"

DR. TOM MULLINS
FOUNDING PASTOR
CHRIST FELLOWSHIP CHURCH
PALM BEACH GARDENS, FLORIDA

"I was deeply moved by *The River*. I found myself captured by the beauty of the story and fully immersed in the characters and their lives. I believe there's a little Gabriel Clarke in all of us. This book is a must read for any stage of life."

BRUCE KOBLISH
PRESIDENT/CEO
THE WORSHIP NETWORK

THE
RIVER

A NOVEL

MICHAEL NEALE

For information, contact:
THE RIVER EXPERIENCE, LLC
2550 Meridian Blvd, Suite 350
Franklin, TN 37067
(615) 373-2500
For bookings, contact: events@theriverexperience.com

For more information, visit: **www.theriverexperience.com**

Cover and Interior Design by KENEDIK Design Studio
International Standard Book Number 978-0-9837879-0-7

11 12 13 14 15 9 8 7 6 5 4 3 2 1

Printed and bound in Canada
by Ellie Claire Gift & Paper Corporation

DEDICATION

To Leah Paige Neale,
my wife, my love,
and my best friend.

CONTENTS

FROM AN ENTRY IN A JOURNAL

I love coming to The River.

The River is magical. It's full of wonder and mystery. For thousands of years, The River has been carving its way through the Earth. As the water pours over the landscape, crashes against the banks, and cascades over the rocks, everything changes in its path. The terrain, the trees, even the wildlife—everything is shaped by The River. Everything in the canyon is at the mercy of The River.

The River is wild, free, and untamable. It's foaming, twisting, and thundering. There are places where the water shoots down into crevices and canyons and creates this amazing thunder, and then there are places where the water settles into pools of complete calm. There are peaceful eddies where the riverbed is flat and the gradient is level, where the water mirrors the beautiful mountains surrounding the landscape. I love being with The River.

The River is alive. The River is timeless, and it's moving all over the world.

I find myself drawn to The River. With its beauty and power, The River calls to me. The River can be known but not fully. Therein lies the mystery. The River has a voice, and I love the way it sounds. When I'm with The River, I just know it's where I'm meant to be. It touches something deep inside my soul. It connects me to a bigger story in some indescribable way. I could spend countless hours just watching and listening.

Since I was a small child, I've been fascinated and captivated by The River. It's mesmerizing really. In many ways, the waters speak to me. Whether I'm skipping stones in a smooth eddy or feeling the thunder of a waterfall, when I'm with The River, I feel alive.

I've experienced The River in many ways in my life. I haven't always understood those experiences. What I will say is that The River has allowed me to feel the deepest grief and given me the greatest joy.

I must confess, though, that there have been times when I've been angry with The River. It doesn't seem to mind. I've been afraid of The River, too, but somehow it keeps drawing me in. I am a small speck compared to its mighty waters, yet The River seems completely aware of me in a cosmic sort of way. Whether I was indifferent, aloof, or passionately bitter, The River never stopped calling me.

I've watched The River from places high in the mountains where you couldn't hear the water's movement. The sight reminded me of a rich Monet hanging on the wall.

I've sat on the banks and listened to the water flowing by gently whispering to me like a mother soothing her child to sleep. I've waded into the calm eddies, where the cool water cascaded over my toes, massaging my feet and invigorating my skin.

To float down the gentle rapids without a raft is like being carried in the strong arms of a father. Love pushes out any fear as you're lifted through the canyon. You feel adventure and safety at the same time.

I've skipped rocks on the mirrored water. I've fly-fished in the deepest gorges and better yet, I've rafted monstrous whitewater in breathtaking canyons all over the world. I'm still learning to trust The River, though, because I don't know all that the waters have in store for me.

But I do know this: I can't live without The River. I'm still fearful yet drawn in. I'm in awe yet completely at home. Somehow, in the deepest places, I feel The River knows I'm here. I can't explain it. I just know. It has never left me, and I will never leave it. I am captured and set free in this beautiful dance of hearts.

I can tell you this from my journey: the more you experience The River, the more you want to stay close by. When you experience The River, you live.

Gabriel Clarke
November 7, 1979

A NOTE FROM THE AUTHOR

If stories come to you, care for them. And learn to give them away where they are needed. Sometimes a person needs a story more than food to stay alive.

—Barry Lopez, in *Crow and Weasel*

———————◆———————

I've always loved to tell stories, especially with friends or family. I love sharing the fun of an unlikely event, a self-deprecating *faux pas*, or a recount of a whimsical conversation with one of my kids. There's nothing like a great story.

My grandfather was a wonderful storyteller. I used to sit next to his wood-burning stove with a Chek root beer float in hand, listening to him tell me about his childhood. He described the hardships of growing up during the Great Depression, how he used to build Goodyear blimps, and how his personally customized RV *always* broke down at the top of some mountain pass in the harshest of winters.

I never really cared whether his stories were based on fact or fiction. I just loved getting lost in the magic of his words. It was as if I could experience those adventures and relationships too, even though I was only eight years old.

The story I'm about to tell you is inspired by a collage of events, conversations, and happenings in my life and the life of my family. I believe you'll find some of your story here as well. I'm not sure how that happens, but it always does.

INTRODUCTION

Every now and then, you have an encounter with someone who simply changes your life. A conversation or interaction so profound, it seems otherworldly. You can't get his (or her) story out of your head and heart.

It's hard to explain how powerful stories can resonate within our hearts on many levels, but it's often because of the way they speak with passion, heartache, or even joy. Maybe it's the way they unknowingly reach into our heart of hearts with their words.

I don't think these encounters happen by chance. I think there is a reason, although we will never understand the full weaving of life's tapestry of events this side of the eternal. I have had such an encounter with someone. It moved me to my core, so much so that I had to share it with you. I'll keep sharing it as long as I have breath. For the next few pages, I'd like you to grab a cup of coffee—or a root beer float—and sit down and let me tell you about a conversation I had with a man named Gabriel Clarke.

It all began when I was traveling back to Nashville from the West Coast. My first flight from LAX landed in Denver at about 6:30 p.m. on a Thursday night, when things at DIA were slowing down a bit. I was feeling exhausted after two days of countless meetings, a lack of rest (I don't sleep well away from home), and the tiring travel.

I'm not sure what it is about planes, but the only way I can describe it is that flying makes me feel stale, grimy, and in need of a teeth cleaning. I got off of my first flight from Los Angeles and approached the monitor to see which gate was handling my connecting flight.

According to my itinerary, I had about fifty minutes until my flight to Nashville took off. The monitor said otherwise. Like a deer staring into oncoming headlights, I stood fixated at the monitor, hoping my glare would supernaturally change the DELAYED message to BOARDING.

Unfortunately, that did not happen. After a quick visit to the restroom, I made the trek to my new gate, dodging the carts carrying the old folks and doing my best to ignore the annoying beeps. When I arrived, I discovered that my flight was not delayed—it was *canceled* due to mechanical issues with the aircraft.

There wasn't much I could do except queue up with a line of agitated passengers waiting to speak with the gate agent. In a very unsympathetic and "get over it" tone, she explained that my only option was to reschedule on a different flight leaving at 10:50 p.m.

I did some quick calculations. With the time change, this would put me in my own bed on our small farm forty-five minutes outside of Nashville at about 3 a.m. Oh joy. I *love* going home, just not in the middle of the night when I'm tiptoeing around like a burglar, trying to keep our chocolate labs from waking the kids.

I took a deep breath and resigned myself to my fate. I had a three-and-a-half-hour rendezvous with the C Concourse in Denver, and there was no way around that. I hunted for a quiet corner where I could spend some time reading and listening to music. It was a rare opportunity for down time, so I figured I'd make the most of it.

About eight gates down, I found an entire section where the lights were dim, the hanging flat-screen TVs were turned off, and the gates were closed. There wasn't a soul in sight. I looked for the best spot and claimed a section of seating in the back corner, next to the windows that looked out over the tarmac. I called my wife and kids to say goodnight and break the news that I wouldn't see them until the morning.

After we said our goodbyes, I immediately reached for my iPod, plugged in my earphones, and shut out the world by listening to my favorite movie scores. I had a spy novel I'd started on the flight from LA, so I pulled the oversized paperback out of my backpack, propped my feet up on the chair across from me, and began reading. After ten pages, though, my solitude and bliss came to an abrupt end.

Out of the corner of my eye, I saw a large character moving

toward me. *Who in the world is heading all the way over here? Surely it's not someone I know from home.* My thoughts were running a mile a minute. Sure enough, this man plopped down two seats from me and opened a canvas bag that looked to be filled with enough camping and hiking gear to scale the Himalayas.

I couldn't believe it. Of all the places in the airport, why would he sit down right next to me? I ignored him, burying my head in my book, but he kept going through his canvas bag, checking his equipment and carrying on a one-sided conversation with himself.

I turned my music up, sighed loudly, and returned to my book, trying to send a message that I wanted to be left alone. Out of the corner of my eye, I noticed that he kept looking over at me again and again. I could tell he was itching for conversation, so I looked up from my book and gave Mountain Man a half-hearted grin.

He was at least six feet tall and built like an Australian rugby player. A long, shaggy beard with disheveled dirty blonde hair poured out from under his army green knit cap. If I had to guess his age, I would say that he was probably in his mid-fifties. Dressed in a worn-thin plaid flannel shirt with rolled-up sleeves and khaki shorts, he wore large hiking boots with thick thermal socks bunched around his ankles. His skin was weathered and tan, his eyes were crystal blue, and his worn face was lined with wrinkles. He looked like he just stepped out of a Discovery Channel documentary.

The older man looked at me and said something. I couldn't

understand him because of the cranked-up music playing in my ears, so I pulled out my earphones. "Sorry, man, but I couldn't hear you. What was that?"

"Heading home or away?"

Not a very deep question. "I'm heading home," I said, hoping my three-word reply would send a hint that I didn't want to be bothered.

He would not be deterred. "Me too. I've been gone for over three months. I'm ready for my own bed." He slouched in his chair and leaned back, staring at the ceiling. I thought maybe our conversation was over, meaning I could get back to my book and music in peace.

Instead, he looked over again. "How long until your flight leaves?"

I knew now that I should just give in, so I closed my book and set it on my lap.

"I have until 10:30," I said, and I told him what happened with the canceled flight to Nashville. He told me that he was early for his red-eye to the East Coast.

From there, we exchanged the typical small talk:

"Where are you from?"

"Where are you going?"

"Weather has been unpredictable, huh?"

All the usual stuff. But with guys, an introductory conversation wouldn't be complete unless you ask, "What do you do?"

I always hate talking about what I do, but it's part of the man language. We feel we can tell a lot about a person by what they do for a living.

So I plunged in. "What do you do for a living?" I asked curiously.

He hedged a little bit. "Well, I like the outdoors a lot, you know." He smiled and looked at me, comfortable with the awkward pause.

"Well, what about this three-month trip you were on? Was it work related, or just R & R?"

"Oh, no," he said through a chuckle. "Not much R & R on this trip. I actually just finished running *National Geographic*'s 'Top Ten Most Dangerous and Beautiful Rivers in the World.' Five continents, 19,000 miles, a couple of near-death experiences, some serious wildlife, tons of new friends, and the time of my life." He looked over at me out of the corner of his eye. "It was outrageous," he said with a bit of a crazed grin.

The conversation became riveting. I found out his name was Gabriel Clarke, a third-generation whitewater guide. For the next several hours, Gabriel regaled me with his life story—the legendary story of where he came from, the defining tragedy of his childhood, the triumph of where he was in life now, and what got him through. The way he energetically explained things, it was as if this was the first time he'd ever told anyone.

His passion was contagious, and by the time he was finished, I was thankful for the interruption that night in the Denver airport. What I'm about to tell you is his story as he told it to me. If you're anything like me, or others who've heard Gabriel's story, then you'll never forget it. You'll never be the same.

I know I'll never be the same—ever.

CHAPTER 1

THE BIG HIKE

On a cool September Sunday in 1956, John Clarke woke up at daybreak wanting to get out of the house and enjoy the outdoors. Being a single father, and not having arranged care for his son Gabriel that day, he decided to take the little guy on a hike into the Firewater gorge at The River.

"Dad! Slow down!" shouted the four-year-old boy in a husky yet high-pitched voice.

"Not too much further, buddy, and then we'll take a break," replied his father. "You're gonna love the view when we get there! Papaw took me here when I was your age, and I never forgot it."

Running out of breath in this flatter section of the trail but still determined, John kept moving. Their final destination was a rarely visited scenic overlook of Splash Canyon from high above Whitefire River. His backpack—filled with trail mix, homemade beef jerky, water, first aid gear and raincoats—must have weighed twenty pounds.

"Dad! Put me up high!" John stopped to wait for Gabriel to catch up, and then with one strong motion, he hoisted the boy onto his shoulders for the rest of the hike. They continued on to the top, father and son united in their love for the raw outdoors.

That's where he felt at home. John knew his way around nature better than his own house. "If I could, I'd live outdoors constantly," he'd tell friends from time to time. At five feet, eleven inches and 189 pounds, John was a rugged thirty-two-year-old built solid and muscular. He was strong as an ox from his years of rock climbing and running The River. Crow's feet were starting to appear outside his blue-grey eyes. With sandy blonde hair in a shag cut and a swagger to boot, he was a man of few words with wisdom beyond his years.

The Clarke family was a cornerstone of Corley Falls, Colorado. His grandfather and father had all but built the entire town on the back of their inn and whitewater adventure camp. John, carrying on the tradition, had assumed the day-to-day operations, which included training the whitewater guides. For nearly thirty-six springs and summers, Big Water Adventure Camp gave rafters and expeditionists an experience they would never forget on the Whitefire River. John Clarke repeated his father's words often: "The Canyon is just a bit of God's art."

The summer rafting season was over. Only a few seasoned kayakers would run The River during this time, so John had a few days off between guided hiking tours and teaching at the Whitewater Guide School his father had started. They had an unusual amount of rain that week, so The River was running particularly high.

The canyon and surrounding forest were completely breathtaking, especially in the early morning hours. The misty fog lifted slowly, leading to a sensation like they were walking in the clouds. Birds chirped in a poly-rhythmic symphony, and one could smell the spruce, fir, and pine trees with arresting potency. Chipmunks scampered about as if they were playing "hide and seek" while making their final sweep of the forest floor for nuts before winter. All manner of wildlife made an appearance at any given time, including bears, wolves, and deer, creating a truly wild and magical place.

"How far are we going, Dad?"

"About a couple more football fields," his father replied. John tried to talk about distances in terms he could picture.

Like a miniature version of his father, Gabriel was a stocky kid with a round face. His straight blonde hair swung back and forth when he walked, but he usually ran everywhere he went. He had eyelashes for days and his sky-blue eyes arrested ladies wherever his father took him. Of course, his dad liked that.

Gabriel was smart, full of questions, and not averse to mischief. His questions would come out of nowhere and often send his father to the floor laughing or make him scratch his head in wonder.

On this morning hike, however, Gabriel's questions were more poignant.

When am I gonna see Mommy again? Sammy Overton said maybe she's mad.

Jackson Wilbur said mommies are important because you need to have a mommy to be borned. Can we go see Mommy today?

John was taken aback by the randomness of the questions, which broke his heart. He knew that it would be at least until Thanksgiving before Gabriel got to see his mother.

Without slowing down, John continued up the rugged path. "Well, buddy, you're gonna get to see your momma real soon. She's not mad at you, Gabe. Don't ever think that. She just lives quite a ways away, so it's hard for her to get here. Hey, look at those chipmunks!"

John knew he was trying to change the subject, and his heart was heavy. The sadness would come over him in waves sometimes. How he wished they were still together! The feelings of despondency would get overwhelming. Usually he'd just distract himself with more work.

John unloaded Gabriel from his shoulders carefully. "Shhhh. Don't scare 'em off." Before John could get the backpack off, the boy was ransacking it for some peanuts. He took a few out of a bag and made his way slowly toward the pair of chipmunks. Without fear, Gabriel held out his hand with a few shelled peanuts resting on his fingertips. Cautiously, both chipmunks approached with quick twitches looking from side to side. They seemed to be trying to get away with something they shouldn't be doing.

"Hold your hand steady," John counseled.

Taking their time, the two chipmunks each grabbed a couple of peanuts and scampered back to the tree.

"Did you see that, Dad?"

"Sure did. You made some new friends. You should name 'em." John zipped up his backpack and loaded it back onto his shoulders. "You ready to go to the top?"

With a stick almost too heavy to hold, Gabriel lifted it like a sword and with the fiercest war cry he could muster, he cried out, "Let's go!"

John loaded him back onto his shoulders, and they resumed their trek to the overlook. For about fifty yards, all they could hear was the sound of John's boots colliding with the trail. The fog was beginning to lift a bit. Gabriel leaned down over his father's face and said, "Nuts and Pea."

"What?" John held a bewildered grin on his face.

"That's their names. Nuts and Pea. Cause they like peanuts. Get it? Pea . . nuts . . . Nuts and Pea!"

John had a good laugh. "That one is going in the book," he said, referring to the journal where he kept a record of milestones, quotes, and stories from his journeys with Gabriel. With the boy's hands resting on his father's head in complete contentment, they moved on.

By now, they could hear the roar of The River. The water rushing over the riverbed sounded like a relentless windstorm— exhilarating, frightening, and calming all at the same time. John turned on a rough path that wound away from The River and toward densely treed forest.

"The River is that way, Dad." Gabriel was pointing to his left and behind him. "Why are we going away from The River?"

"Don't lean backwards. You're making it harder than it is." The father paused. "Just wait, buddy. A couple more minutes, and you'll see."

The River made a hard right turn, and around the corner, cliffs jutted out, creating the most spectacular waterfall in the region in Firewater Canyon. They could almost feel The River moving the ground. The air was misty with the spray.

They came through the final patch of trees, and as the path curled to their left, it was as if a curtain lifted, showing the stage for the first time.

"Wow! Awesome! Look at that, Dad!"

"I know. Isn't that amazing, bud?" He took Gabriel off his shoulders and then walked over to a tree about ten feet from a jagged slope that overlooked the edge of The River. "You see this tree, buddy?" John placed his hand on the bark. "You don't go past this tree. It's very dangerous, and Daddy doesn't want you to fall into The River. Got that?"

Distracted and looking down the canyon, Gabriel nodded.

With his hand on top of Gabriel's head, John turned him like a puppet so he had to look him in the eye.

"Understand?"

"Yeah, Dad."

Directly across the gorge, the canyon walls rose sharply. They were covered with picturesque reddish rock and hundreds of spruce, fir, and pine trees pointing straight to the sky like giant pencils. Rocks had fallen off the sides of the canyon over thousands of years to create mini-mountains in The River's flow.

Millions of gallons of water pounded the gorge every minute, falling three stories before hitting the first level of rock pile. The water continued cascading three more levels, each about ten feet in height. At the bottom of the falls, the water splashed back up in a massive circular motion due to a large hole in the riverbed. The effect was like a giant washing machine—a suckhole is what the guides at Big Water Adventure Camp called it.

John took off his backpack and grabbed a couple of water bottles. "Here, buddy. You need to drink some water to stay hydrated. It's pretty dry at these altitudes, and your body needs lots of fluids."

They both sat down on a log, where John unpacked some homemade jerky.

Gabriel was gnawing on a piece when he suddenly announced that he wanted to go into the water.

John chuckled. "You'd freeze, bud! That water is ice cold."

"But it looks fun!"

"It's fun all right, but not when it's this cold and not in falls that big. Maybe downstream, where it's calm, I'll let you put your feet in. Maybe I'll teach you how to skip rocks."

John took out a worn leather pouch full of vintage Bennington marbles and held them up. In the background, the constant roar of The River was pounding.

"Ready to play?"

"Yeah!" Gabriel shouted.

John had a large collection of vintage marbles that had been passed down from his grandfather to him. John cleared a place in the dirt and drew up a playing circle.

"I'm gonna beat you this time, Dad!"

"Ha! We'll see, little man!"

It was a few minutes before 9 a.m., and the sun was burning through a cloud cover. As John crouched down, though, he heard voices off in the distance.

"Who in the world is out here?" John glanced over his shoulder at The River. "Stay here," he directed.

John quickly walked to the edge of the cliff, where he could see more of The River upstream. The voices shouting back and forth were sporadic at best. He couldn't make out what they were saying, so he climbed down the slope to a plateau that jutted out over The River. Looking upstream, he spotted a young guy sitting in a kayak that had stalled in a small eddy next to the riverbank. He was shouting something upstream.

John's heart sank because he knew what was happening. He shouted to get the young man's attention.

"Do not ride! Huge falls! Do not ride! Huge falls!"

The kayaker couldn't hear him.

"What are you doing, Dad?" Gabriel stood at the top of the slope.

"Just stay there! I've got to go a little lower and tell them." Looking back at Gabriel, he emphatically said, "You stay there!"

A pair of other kayakers came into view, but they were at least two hundred yards away from John. These guys obviously did not know the terrain. These rapids were Level VI. This water was not navigable, even by the most experienced kayakers.

John knew this would mean certain serious injury or death for these unprepared adventurers. He was hoping they would have the sense to stop and scout the terrain.

John edged closer to The River, his heart racing from the dangers these two young men were facing. They were laughing and having a jolly time with no clue of what was ahead. John slid down on the pebbled slope, bracing himself with his left arm and coming to a stop on a ledge about twenty feet from the water. He took off his outer hiking vest, and like a flagman at the finish line of an auto race, he began waving it and shouting frantically, "Danger! Danger! Danger!"

He saw the first kayaker coming down The River. Hoping he would get his attention, he kept waving and shouting. Finally, just before the point of no return, the kayaker looked up and saw John. He immediately changed direction and steered himself out of the main flow of water into an eddy on the other side of The River.

John shouted, "Are there more of you coming?"

The kayaker cupped his ear and called back. "What? Say again!"

About that time, another kayaker came around the bend in The River. The first kayaker tried to get his attention as John kept waving frantically. The second guy sported a wide grin on his face and was hooting and hollering. He stayed in the center of the moving waters as the rapids picked up and The River's gradient began to drop. He passed his friend and entered the whitewater flow. There was nowhere else to pull out. It was inevitable. He was going over the falls.

The first drop was more than three stories high with jagged rocks on either side. The water then poured over and around a giant boulder in the middle of The River, only to fall an additional ten or fifteen feet. At the bottom of the second falls was a massive crevice in the riverbed, where the churning water created a huge suckhole.

At this point, all John and the other kayaker could do was watch. The pale yellow kayak launched off the first massive fall and quickly disappeared under the mist and thunder of water. John's heart was in his throat. A few seconds passed, and suddenly, the kayaker popped out—but upside down—like a fishing bobber.

John sprung into action. He scrambled down the slope to intercept the kayak before the next set of falls and rapids. He reached the riverbank as the kayak floated past him—still upside down—with a man trapped under water, probably knocked unconscious from the first fall.

John glanced back up the hillside and saw Gabriel holding on to a tree, watching the scene unfold. John motioned to him. "Get back, Gabe! Get back!"

Gabriel froze, hugging the tree, not letting his father out of sight.

"Just hang on, buddy. I'll be up in a minute to get you! Stay right there!" John turned back around to see the kayak take a glancing blow from a boulder in The River and plunge over the next fall. Long seconds passed before there was any sign of him. His friend was stuck on the other side of the stream, unable to help.

John made his way swiftly to the bottom of the falls, in time to see the kayak emerge from the foaming water. The kayak had been pinned under the falls, kept down by the relentless water, but now the upside-down kayak floated to a rock on the side nearest to John.

The water, still deep and moving swiftly, pressed the kayak against the rock with great force. John shot a glance back up hill to check on Gabriel while he tried to figure what he could do. He knew this kayaker might have a shot at survival if he could pull him out in the next few seconds or so.

Holding on to a tree with his right hand and reaching with his left foot, he almost touched the tip of the kayak. His plan was to dislodge the kayak from the rock and pull it out in calmer water. He leaned out, but the kayak was just too far. John grabbed a dead branch and struck the kayak, but the force of the water was too strong to dislodge it. Without a life vest, he knew he had to be supremely cautious.

"D-a-d-d-y! D-a-d-d-y!" John faintly heard Gabriel's call, but he was concentrating on the kayak. He couldn't bear to watch a man die right in front of him. Torn between staying on the shore versus risking his life for the rescue, with precious seconds ticking by and one last glance up to Gabriel, John jumped out onto the kayak, bear-hugged it, but struggled to hold on. He tried to kick his foot up on the rock to push the kayak back enough to move it around the rock.

Gabriel's shout turned to a scream. "D-a-d-d-y! C-o-m-e b-a-c-k!"

After a few moments of struggle, John couldn't hold on

anymore. He took one huge breath and disappeared under the greenish blue water. In just a few seconds, he pushed off another rock on the river bottom, and the kayak was freed. The craft righted itself and quickly floated downstream.

Seconds ticked by turning into minutes, but John did not surface. The force of water had pinned him under the rock.

Gabriel screamed louder for his father. "The boat is free! There it goes! Daddy! There it goes!"

Meanwhile, the first kayaker had gotten out of his kayak and scramble down the riverbank to the bottom of the falls. He reached his buddy, who appeared to be cold, blue, and lifeless.

He quickly pulled him out and laid him on a rock and started mouth-to-mouth breathing to revive him. Miraculously, he was able to get a pulse again.

———————◆◈◆———————

Gabriel watched it all unfold. His four-year-old mind couldn't comprehend how long a man could survive underwater. He continued to clutch the tree, calling out to his father.

"Daddy! They made it out! You can come back now!"

He shifted his focus downstream, where the man was caring for the lifeless kayaker. Maybe his father was swimming and would show up down there.

But he never did.

His dad never came back.

His father was gone. His hero just disappeared.

No more games of marbles.

No goodbyes.
No hugs.
Just gone.

CHAPTER 2

~ LIFE IN KANSAS ~

"Gabriel, come on! Breakfast is ready!"

The smell of frying bacon and eggs saturated the one-bedroom rental attached to the back of an old farmhouse in Cairo, Kansas. Gabriel and his mother, Maggie, ate bacon and eggs a lot because they lived on a farm that belonged to Earl and Vonda Cartwright.

The Cartwrights were very generous to the young mother and son. Their dingy white, turn-of-the-century farmhouse sat in the middle of 113 acres of cornfields. As far as the eye could see, flat fields of mature corn stalks grew six and seven feet high. In addition to a garden lined with rows of lettuce, cucumbers, and tomatoes, the Cartwrights kept a couple of cows for milk, several pigs, and a chicken coop crowded with thirty-six hens that yielded dozens of eggs every day. They sold their extra eggs and vegetables at a farmer's market in town a couple of days a week.

Every few days, Mister Earl—as Maggie and Gabriel called him—would leave a paper bag of vegetables and a carton of eggs on their doorstep. A couple times a month, there'd be a whole chicken in the grocery bag, too. If it weren't for the Cartwrights' generosity, Maggie's cupboard would be bare several days a month. Her tips from the Cairo Diner were slight and barely covered their basic needs for food and shelter or the gas for her 1952 Ford pickup.

The modest rental behind the main house had its own entrance, a small stove and sink, a 10x10 living area, and one bedroom and bath. The place was tiny but enough for a mom and her son.

One morning at quarter past six, eight-year-old Gabriel rolled out of a miniature cot covered by well-worn patchwork quilts. Donning a pair of faded plaid pajama pants that were six inches too short and a faded T-shirt that he'd nearly worn out over the last year, Gabriel stumbled out of the bedroom he shared with his mother and sat down at the table without a sound. His disheveled white-blond hair was matted down like straw found in Mister Earl's barn, and his eyes were swollen from another night of tear-filled sleep.

His mom kept up a steady patter as she prepared breakfast. "You don't have much time, baby. You need to eat. We gotta leave for school real soon. I'm gonna bake you a cake tonight. Somebody has a birthday today! I can't believe you're eight already!"

She checked to see if his countenance had changed. It hadn't.

"Hey, Sammy's mom told me at the diner that the boys were gonna go fishing again today down at The Pond. You should join 'em. Don't you think that would be fun?"

The local pond was a favorite place for the boys in town. Whether it was fishing or swimming on a hot summer day, hanging out under the trees, or building forts made with fallen branches, if you were a boy in Cairo, you knew about The Pond. Gabriel didn't respond and kept eating his cereal. Frustrated by her inability to connect, she asked him, "Why don't you want to go have fun with the other boys?"

No response.

Wiping her hands on her apron, she knelt down beside him. Gabriel remained focused on his corn flakes as if she weren't there. "Baby, you gotta have some fun. Go play! I want you to go with the boys."

He shook his head slowly, took his last bite, and scurried to the bathroom and slammed the door.

Gabe!" she cried out with desperation and worry. She put her ear up to the bathroom door. "It's gonna be alright. You'll have a lot of fun," she said with a quiver in her voice. She rapped her knuckles on the bathroom door. "Gabriel? Gabriel!" she said, even louder. "Okay, sweetie, I know you're in your secret place."

She paused and took a deep breath. "It's okay."

Maggie knew that today would be one of those hard days. Not sure what to do next, she heard a soft knock at the door. Miss Vonda was peering through the dusty screen door. Normally a quiet woman who kept to herself, she was a petite but round woman in her early seventies with rosy cheeks, a pile of salt and pepper grey hair pulled up in a bun, and a hearty disposition. Maggie always found her reserved but kind.

On this particular morning, she was wearing one of her two home-sewn farm dresses, both in light blue. She wore one during the week for farm chores; the other one was reserved for Sunday church.

"Here's some fresh milk from Little Cow." Her dairy cows didn't have real names. They were just known as Little Cow and Big Cow. Maggie tried to gather herself a bit as she approached the door. "Mornin', Miss Vonda." She blotted her tear-swollen eyes.

Miss Vonda always seemed to have a smile on her face. "You got enough food?" That was Miss Vonda's answer to everything. She loved to cook.

"We're okay," Maggie replied. "Thank you though."

There was a bit of an awkward pause until Miss Vonda asked tenderly, "Is he in his secret place today?"

Maggie couldn't hold her feelings in any longer. With a flood of emotion, she began to weep. "I don't know what to do! I just want my boy to get better, you know? He's having those terrible dreams again. He barely says two words on the hard days. I just want him to be a regular boy. I want him to live, really live! I'm just not sure I can take this much more."

"There, there, Maggie. Tomorrow will be a better day. Let me help you with your dishes."

On his better days, Gabriel would converse more and seem to escape whatever fears and thoughts were tormenting him. He especially liked it when Mister Earl would give him rides on his red tractor, but that only happened during certain times of the year.

During his hard days, though, he would not talk. Instead, he would retreat to his "secret place"—a place he liked to go whenever he was afraid or sad. The secret place might be the bedroom he and his mom shared, it might be the bathroom, or it might be sitting on the big red tractor in the barn. That was his favorite spot to get away, and he would spend hours hanging around the tractor on the hard days. The secret place was his haven of safety, a bubble where he could survive the memories of watching his father die and the feelings of great loss and abandonment.

He'd been living with his mother for four years since The River took his dad. Before the tragic accident, he'd see his mother only at holiday times when his father took him to see her.

Now it was just he and his mom, and while he knew she loved him, there was still a huge hole in his heart. The memories of times with his father were few but strong. He could still picture his father instructing new rafters before their first run or telling of his exploits over dinner. Most of all, he remembered how strong he was when he would pick him up with one arm and say, "How'd you get so big?"

She was too young to understand that John loved her very much. They had tried to make it work when she was pregnant and for the first eight months after Gabriel was born. Gabriel wasn't supposed to happen, but one night of passion turned into a little life that she couldn't take care of. She was so young and terrified, which is why she left Gabriel in care of his father. She fled Colorado and moved back to Kansas where she was from. Then the horrible news of John's death changed everything, and she was suddenly thrust into the responsibility of raising a broken boy scarred by the loss of his father. Waves of guilt washed over her daily, and questions relentlessly haunted her.

What would have happened if I stayed?

Why did I run?

Why did he have to die?

Tons of regrets filled her heart. Would things have changed if they had been together that fateful day? Would John still be alive today?

She really didn't know what to do about Gabriel. He didn't talk much at all, even on his better days. He was sad most of the time. He was barely making it in school, and he refused to play baseball or go to The Pond with the boys. Gabriel was scared of his own shadow, a shy and timid kid who woke up in the middle of the night crying but he would never say why. She assumed he was upset from the trauma of the accident, but she wasn't sure. She just wanted to know her boy was going to be okay.

Since the accident three years ago, she couldn't get him out of this dark place he seemed to be living in. To see a little boy who was so sad seemed unnatural and weighed on Maggie every minute of every day. He was locked inside some kind of emotional prison, and she couldn't find the key.

After they finished the dishes, Miss Vonda said, "I better go pull some eggs. I'll check in with you later."

Maggie made her way back over to the bathroom door. "Gabe . . . sweetie . . . we have to leave for school. I can't be late for work again."

There was no response. She opened the unlocked door to find Gabriel sitting on the floor with his back up against the old bear claw tub. His small arms were wrapped around knees that were tucked up under his chin. He was staring at the floor, disconsolate.

Maggie walked over and sat next to him. She could see that his eyes were red around the edges. Mother and son sat in silence for a couple of minutes, then she reached out and patted his left arm gently. "I like to go to my secret places, too. We're gonna get through this, baby. We're gonna get through this . . . come on."

She stood up, put her hands underneath his arms, and helped him to his feet. Usually when the hard days came, Maggie would just get upset, which led to a sense of frustration because she couldn't figure out how to help him. On this particular day, though, she had an unusual measure of patience. She walked with him into the bedroom and helped him get his clothes on for school. After he was dressed, they returned to the bathroom, where she washed his face with a cold rag and helped him comb his hair.

She continued her one-sided conversation:

"Maybe today you'll get to sit next to that pretty little girl Jenny . . . you want me to ask your teacher about that?"

She finally got a little grin from Gabriel, which gave her hope that maybe this day would transform from a hard day to a better day. "Why don't you go play marbles while I get ready?"

Gabriel had a worn leather pouch of old Bennington marbles that he used to play with his dad. He kept them underneath his cot. He liked to sort his marble collection by color and type. He knew all about the different kinds of marbles: Alleys, Aggies, Chinas, plasters, and turtles. Playing marbles reminded him of his father, and that made him feel good.

As she was walking into the bathroom, Gabriel finally broke his silence.

"Maybe I could go to The Pond after school. Maybe they'll want to play marbles. Can I take my Benningtons? I bet they'd really like those."

Maggie's eyebrows rose on her face. She could hardly contain her joy.

"Uh . . . yeah, I'm sure they'd play marbles with you. We'll go right after school, okay?"

She quickly closed the door to the bathroom and broke into tears. This time they were tears of joy. Maybe they had turned a corner. Maybe this would help Gabriel out of his shell. Maybe a visit to The Pond would help him come alive.

She didn't know much about religion, but she looked up to the ceiling and kept whispering over and over, "Thank you, thank you, thank you."

CHAPTER 3

⚛ THE POND ⚛

The cornfields were maturing on this steaming hot day in late August, with probably less than a month to go before harvest time.

The year was 1959. There was a lot going on in the world at the time. Jet airliners were taking people across the ocean. NASA had just launched the first monkey into space, a squirrel monkey named Baker. The motion picture *Ben Hur* was being shown in 70mm Panavision in big cities, and sometimes folks in Cairo would make the two-and-a-half-hour drive to St. Louis and pay the princely sum of $1 per ticket to see the blockbuster film, but that was rare.

Mostly, none of that city slicker stuff mattered much in Cairo. Everything in this farming town of 250 revolved around corn, the feed and seed store, Sunday church, and the Cairo Diner. Cairo was quiet, sleepy, and safe. Crime was nearly nonexistent. Occasionally, you'd hear that Jimmy Bly was caught stealing penny gum from the Five & Dime, but that was about it. The rumor was that Jimmy didn't even like gum. He kiped gum to create a little adventure in his life.

Leather-skinned farmers with denim overalls and dirt-streaked white T-shirts hung around the diner in the late afternoon, enjoying a cup of coffee and the latest gossip. The conversation usually hinged around how the corn yield was looking, what the weatherman on KMOX radio was predicting, or how well the cows were producing. Every now and then, they'd talk about their tractor breakdowns, too.

School got out at 3:20 p.m. that Friday afternoon. At least a couple dozen boys were going to The Pond, something they did every Friday until winter arrived. Situated a mile south of Main Street, The Pond was surrounded on three sides by mature corn stalks and on the fourth by two cottonwood trees reaching at least eighty feet tall. The trees were great for climbing and gave incredible shade.

Throughout the summer, The Pond was the place to be for swimming races, mud wrestling matches, and lots and lots of fishing.

To get there, some boys would walk. Others would ride their bikes. Some of the boys would get dropped off by their moms and walk home at dinnertime. There was six-year-old little Will Rambling. He was small but scrappy. A freckled redhead full of piss and vinegar, he picked fights with the older ones just to see if he could whip them.

James Roy Holly was the ten-year-old expert fisherman.

He was quiet and kind and averse to getting into wrestling matches. Everybody watched how he fished because he always caught the most.

Of course, Jimmy Bly was one of the leaders. He was older and outspoken—and quite the storyteller. He didn't have book smarts, but he knew the way of the world. Or so he thought. He would make up games for everyone to play. Legend had it that twelve-year-old Jimmy once kissed a girl behind the abandoned barn on the edge of town.

J.J. Hopper named himself General J.J. He was the clown of the bunch. Well over five feet tall and every bit of 200 pounds, J.J.'s cheeks were always pushed out like a giant chipmunk from pieces of hard candy in his mouth. He would take on two or three boys in the wrestling matches, but his outclassed and underweight opponents always ended up crying for mercy. Everybody loved General J.J.

The Pond was what all the boys looked forward to—a place where they were in charge. There were no girls to worry about and no parents to tell them to do chores. For a few hours every Friday, they were a part of a tribe and members of a brotherhood.

***

Maggie saw Gabriel coming out of school, swinging his lunch pail and skipping his feet. She knew that when he had his head up and a smile on his face that meant it was a better day. Wearing his favorite black canvas sneakers with the white toe, old denims from the Five & Dime, and his favorite John Deere tractor T-shirt that Mister Earl gave him, Gabriel sprinted toward his mom's truck.

"Hey, Sweetie!" Maggie said. "You had a good day?"

Snapping the door handle three times to get it to open, Gabriel replied, "Hi, Mom. Mrs. Chesley let me show the class my marble collection today. Umm . . . they really liked them."

"Way to go, young man!" She manhandled the column shifter into first gear, let out the stiff clutch, and they chugged away from school.

"I brought you an old shirt to wear to The Pond. You hungry? Here's a peanut butter sandwich too." Maggie hoped that this might be looked upon as the day that ended the hard days.

"Maybe we could just go home. I'm kinda tired."

Maggie saw that his countenance had changed. She restrained her first reaction, which was to pressure him or convince him that everything would be okay. Learning from her past attempts, she knew that any reaction from her would just drive Gabriel deeper into his own fear and insecurity. She just stayed quiet.

Gabriel broke the silence. "I don't know. They said they were doing swimming races, but I don't want to do that."

"Maybe you could show them how to play marbles," Maggie offered. "You could be the first young man to hold marble tournaments at The Pond."

Gabriel looked over and smiled a bit. "You think so?"

"Sure, I do. I'll come back later and check on you. Plus

Jimmy will be there. You like Jimmy's stories don't you?"

Gabriel took a deep breath and nodded his head. As they arrived at the edge of town, Maggie turned down the old dirt road that would take them to The Pond. She couldn't see The Pond from the dirt road because of the high corn stalks, but there was no mistaking the towering cottonwood trees.

As they pulled off the road, she heard the high-pitched voices of boys who had already arrived. They were yelling and laughing.

Gabriel had finished eating one-half of his peanut butter sandwich. He started to open the door.

"Hang on, baby. Look here." Maggie licked her thumb and began to wipe off the peanut butter from around his mouth. "Don't forget your marbles."

Gabriel reached in his school bag and pulled out a large mason jar of his favorite marbles. "I'll see you in a little bit, Mom."

"Okay, baby. Be careful."

Gabriel got out of the truck and walked down the path between the cornstalks. Just before he was out of sight, Maggie shouted, "Have fun, Gabe!"

In her heart, she was thrilled that he would be playing with other boys, but she was also worried sick at the same time. She watched him every step of the way until her son disappeared behind the cornstalks.

As Gabriel got closer to The Pond, he nervously ducked into the corn stalks and peered through them to watch the boys. A few were climbing the lower limbs of the largest cottonwood, and two boys were swimming in The Pond and splashing each other.

James Roy Holly and a fishing buddy had brought their sugar cane poles and were baiting their hooks on the other side of The Pond. General J.J. was having trouble with his bike—his chain appeared to be off. He kept kicking the bike and swearing.

Gabriel knew he was on the outside of the tribe. He wasn't sure how he could belong. He heard voices of several boys approaching his way. He ducked down inside the thicket of cornstalks, hoping they wouldn't see him.

They saw him anyway.

"Gabriel, is that you in there?" The voice belonged to Dickie Colter, an eight-year-old know-it-all who constantly ran his mouth.

"Hey guys, look! Gabriel is hiding in the corn! You scared or somethin'? You tryin' to spy on us? I think we should get him, guys!"

Gabriel froze, terrified of what might happen.

"Shut up, Dickie," a husky voice said matter-of-factly. It was Jimmy Bly. "Come on out, man. He's just full of hot air. We're gonna have some fun today!"

Jimmy motioned to him to follow—and that's all it took. Instantly, Gabriel was in the tribe. His fear subsided and his courage increased.

He stumbled out of the cornstalks with his jar of marbles and fell in behind five other boys following the great Jimmy Bly.

When they arrived at The Pond, Jimmy shouted, "Everybody gather 'round! We've got a special event today. We're having a root beer tournament!"

He reached into his denim overalls pocket and pulled out two fistfuls of barrel-shaped root beer candies and placed them on top of a tree stump. "Yeah, baby! Woo-hoo! General J.J. can't play! He always wins!"

Shouts and cheers rose up from all members of the tribe. Most boys couldn't afford treats like root beer barrels very often. The fact that this candy was probably stolen made the game that much more exciting.

The tribe gathered around to listen to Jimmy's instructions. "Okay, everyone. It's mud wrestling day."

All the boys cheered. "General J.J. will referee since he killed everyone last time. J.J., here's a couple of root beers for you as payment for your services." Jimmy tossed the bite-sized candies to him. General J.J. smiled and immediately unwrapped both pieces, shoving the candies into his mouth like he hadn't eaten in months.

The boys discussed who would wrestle whom. James Roy Holly and the other fisherman put their poles down and came running. Gabriel enjoyed the banter, but he certainly didn't want to wrestle, not in the muddy shores of The Pond. There was good, fresh mud since the small lake had receded a bit due to a dry spell in Cairo. What was left was dark, moist mud—

perfect for wrestling.

Jimmy drew a big circle in the mud with a diameter that ran about fifteen paces across. The boys, naturally, gathered around for the first match.

Two of the smaller boys, Henry and Jamie, had climbed one of the cottonwoods for a bird's eye view of the action. At six years of age, they weren't ready for the big wrestling matches, but they loved being around the bigger boys.

Gabriel wanted to avoid wrestling, so he set his jar of marbles in a dense mulberry bush next to one of the cottonwood trees. He certainly did not want anyone stealing his most prized possession. Then he hopped up on the first branch.

"General J.J., would you please introduce our first contestants," Jimmy shouted, using his best announcer voice.

General J.J. held his right arm up to get everyone's attention. "Today's first match will be . . . " He paused for effect. "Little Will versus Dickie Colter!"

Everybody cheered because they knew this would be a great tussle. Little Will was the feistiest six-year-old around, and Dickie Colter was the mouthy mean kid. Each had something to prove, which were the makings of a perfect pond battle.

At this point, Gabriel was so excited to be there that he couldn't stop giggling. He looked up and saw Henry and Jamie on branches at least twenty feet above the ground. Gabriel was scared to climb up that high, but he thought if first-graders could do it, then he could, too.

As the boys were getting ready to begin the match, Gabriel started to climb up higher. He walked his legs up the trunk, telling himself not to look down. Once he reached the level of Henry and Jamie, though, he looked down and immediately became paralyzed with fear. A fall from this height would not be good.

Gabriel came to rest between the massive trunk and the branch the boys were sitting on. They motioned to him to come on out, but he looked down again. The branch hung over the water, which frightened Gabriel even more.

"Gabriel! Let me know when you're ready," yelled Jimmy. "You'll be the scorekeeper, okay?"

Gabriel didn't even respond as he clutched the broad branch with everything he had. He lay on his stomach and tried to shimmy out like a snake. As he was inching his way toward the boys, he became more and more afraid. His palms became sweaty, and he began to visualize what might happen if he fell into The Pond.

Gabriel was terrified of the water. He had learned to swim as a little boy, but he hadn't been in the water since his father drowned. Down below, the boys were cheering and having a great time as the combatants in the first match squared off.

Gabriel reached out to brace himself on a small twig. As he tried to pull himself closer to the boys, he placed his right foot on a small branch for leverage. In an instant, the twig snapped, causing Gabriel to lose his balance. In the blink of an eye, Gabriel found himself dangling from the branch, holding on for dear life with just his hands—a good twenty feet in the air.

"Help! Help!" Gabriel cried out.

By this time, all the boys on the ground saw what was

happening. General J.J. yelled, "Just drop into The Pond, man!"

Dickie taunted him. "What are you scared of, Gabriel? You sound like my little sister!"

Jimmy called out, "Hang on, Gabriel. I'm coming." He rushed over to the tree and began scaling it.

Gabriel screamed, "I can't hang on much longer!"

Six-year-old Henry, who was sitting on the same branch just a few feet away, made his way toward Gabriel by scooting on his seat, inch by inch. He was reaching for Gabriel's hand when the unthinkable happened. Henry lost his balance and fell like a rag doll, bouncing off another branch and splashing into The Pond. It all happened so fast.

Gabriel, momentarily distracted, lost his grip and fell into The Pond right on top of him. In a panic, he flailed his arms in an effort to stay above the water.

The boys responded immediately. General J.J. and Jimmy dove into The Pond to fish the boys out. J.J. was strong enough to pull Gabriel to the shore.

Gabriel, who had ingested water, was coughing and hacking—and crying uncontrollably.

"Where's Henry?" yelled one of the boys in the midst of the pandemonium.

"I haven't found him!" Jimmy yelled.

Several more boys ran into The Pond to join the search in the dark water. Jimmy dove down again, but this time he was successful. He cradled Henry, who was coughing and spitting up water. Jimmy pulled him onto the bank, where the other boys gathered around to see if their friend was all right.

The boys were shell-shocked at the turn of events. Through his tears, Gabriel said, "I'm so sorry. I'm so sorry. I just wanted to watch." He continued to gasp for air so that he could control his crying.

"Are you an idiot?" Dickie asked. "You almost killed him! Why are you even here?"

As Dickie turned and started walking away, he mumbled to J.J., "That kid is worthless."

"Shut up, Dickie!" General J.J. growled at him. He turned to Gabriel and patted his shoulder. "It's okay, man. It wasn't your fault."

Gabriel knew otherwise. Henry had almost died trying to help him, and that prompted great shame.

He knew his first real effort to conquer his fear and connect with the boys of Cairo was a disaster. They wouldn't be seeing him again at The Pond. It was safer to stick close to home—in his secret place.

There was no way he could take a chance on hurting anyone else. He was angry at the water. He was angry with himself.

Better, though, to keep everything to himself.

Risk was not an option anymore.

CHAPTER 4

⟋ Corn Dogs and Marbles ⟍

"Has anyone seen Gabriel this morning?"

Maggie dropped by the Cartwrights' front door to ask if they had seen her son.

Mister Earl got up from the dining room table to greet Maggie. "Last I seen him, he was milling around in the barn," he replied as he swiped at the biscuit crumbs on his shirt. "He was chasing some little critter around."

"That boy hasn't eaten yet, and it's about time to leave," Maggie said with a little agitation in her voice.

"Gabriel!" She paused to listen from the Cartwrights' front porch. "Gabriel Clarke, you need to come eat. It's time to leave!" That's when she saw her son running from the back of the barn and bound up the front porch steps.

"Hi, Mom," he said nonchalantly. They walked through the front door, and Maggie watched Gabriel march to the

Cartwrights' dinner table and put one of Miss Vonda's biscuits in his mouth and the other in his pocket. Then he blitzed toward the front door again.

"And where do you think you're going?" his mother asked.

"Back out to play."

"Don't you remember? We're going to the farmer's market with Mister Earl and Miss Vonda."

"Great! I'll go wait in the truck."

Miss Vonda stepped out of the kitchen after rinsing the last of the breakfast dishes. She always packed a picnic basket of food for the trip to the farmer's market. It was only about an hour away, but Miss Vonda made it her mission in life to make sure nobody ever got too hungry. Maggie knew she usually packed homemade rolls and jam, apples, sliced cucumbers, and carrots from the garden.

It was 7:20 a.m. and time for them to roll out on a calm and cool morning in early October. The sun was breaking through a few scattered clouds and warming the day slowly but surely.

Every few weeks or so Mister Earl, Miss Vonda, Maggie, and Gabriel would load up the old pickup and make the trip of discovery and adventure a few towns over to the All County Farmer's Market. This outing was always a highlight for Gabriel and one of the few times he experienced life outside of school or the farm. This was his education that there was a lot more going on out there than he knew about.

Farmers from all over the county were there, selling their fresh fruits and vegetables, but the farmer's market was much more than that. There were quilt-makers, livestock auctions, clogging competitions, woodworkers, and corn dogs that were to die for. Some folks rented space to sell their knickknacks or stuff they no longer wanted.

On this Saturday morning, the Cartwrights and Maggie made their way out of the screen door as it slammed behind them. They didn't need to lock up the house; this was Cairo. They walked down the front porch steps and headed to the truck.

Gabriel was already sitting in the truck bed with his legs crossed, finishing off his last biscuit. He just looked at Mister Earl, gave one nod of his head, and smiled. Mister Earl got in the driver's side and waited while the two ladies opened the passenger door. Miss Vonda got in first, hoisting her stout frame up while holding her basket of goodies. Maggie, wearing one of her white farm dresses with the small blue flowers, got in next. She had a natural beauty and grace about her. With her tan skin, brown eyes, and long dirty blonde hair, she always got a lot of looks from the men at the market, but she didn't pay much attention. Mister Earl cranked up the truck and put it in gear.

"Good day for the market," he said to anyone who would listen. He popped the clutch, and away they went down the bumpy driveway. Before they made it off of the farm, Gabriel poked his head into the passenger window, his hair blowing in the breeze.

"Can I get a corn dog today?" he asked loudly.

"Yes," replied his mother. "Now sit down before you fall out." Maggie smiled contentedly as they made their way to the main road.

After their seventy-minute rumble through rolling farmsteads, they arrived at the farmer's market. It was just nearing nine o'clock in the morning, and there was already a good crowd.

Gabriel stood up in the back of the truck, peering over the cab with excitement as they parked their car in a dusty field. Some of the exhibitors had set up their booths in the covered areas, while others just backed up their trucks in a row and sold their goods from the tailgate.

There were about eight rows of open-air buildings and a covered livestock area where cows, pigs, chickens and other domestic animals were sold. Depending on which way the wind blew, though, visitors smelled either livestock or the heaven-sent fragrance of corn dogs in the fryer.

Maggie was grateful that Gabriel was now having more good days than bad ones. Life still wasn't easy for them, but days like this one made the journey worth the struggle.

As soon as Mister Earl put the truck in park, Gabriel jumped out and ran ahead.

"Wait for us, Gabriel!" Maggie shouted with a grin on her face.

"Well, somebody's excited today," Miss Vonda said as she scooted down the bench seat.

"Come on, Ma!" Mister Earl said with an impatient tone.

Miss Vonda just glared at him. It took her a little longer due to her short stature. They made their way to the first row of buildings to take in the sights and see what treasures they might find.

They spent the first part of the morning wandering through the livestock barn and watching the steer auction. Then they made their way to Miss Vonda's favorite area, the Quilt Shack. The handmade quilts were so elaborate and perfect that one would think that the whole idea of quilts originated with the All County Farmer's Market.

"I love the way it smells in here," Gabriel said as he breathed in deeply, lifting his nose in the air. He often commented that these ladies smelled like cinnamon and that he wondered if you had to have your hair in a bun to make quilts.

"I'm going to the vegetables," Mister Earl announced. He could take only so much of the arts and crafts section. "Gabriel, you want to pick out some beans?"

Gabriel immediately looked at his mom to see what she'd say.

"Stay close to Mister Earl," Maggie said firmly. Gabriel jumped at the chance to spend time with Mister Earl. He reminded him of Grandpa Isaac, a stern and strong man who ran the Big Water Camp back in Corley Falls.

Gabriel and Mister Earl spent a solid hour looking at all the fresh vegetables and picking out two pounds of green beans. Gabriel loved to snap the beans to check for freshness. After they finished loading their haul into the back of the truck, they headed back to catch the clogging competition. They knew that's where they'd find Miss Vonda and Maggie.

They found them in the last row as the final act, the Cottonwood Cloggers, took the stage. They were the best around. Most people said they always won because they put the cutest kids in front. Everybody cheered wildly as they finished their impressive routine.

"Mom. Mom. Mom!" Gabriel got louder and louder as he yanked on Maggie's sleeve. "Can we get a corn dog now?" He didn't seem to care about seeing who won the clogging competition. His stomach was growling, and the smell of fried corn dogs filled the air.

"Let's wait to see who wins," said his mother. "They're getting ready to make the announcement now."

The master of ceremonies came on the loudspeaker. "And the blue ribbon goes to . . . the Cottonwood Cloggers!" Gabriel gave a half-hearted clap or two and then grabbed Maggie's arm.

"Mom, I'm starving!"

Okay, we're going," Maggie replied.

The four of them made their way over to Cappy's Corn Dogs, always a highlight of the trip. Cappy, a skinny man in his seventies with wrinkled skin and sunken cheeks, had been selling his tasty corn dogs at the All County Farmer's Market for seventeen years. Nobody was sure if Cappy could eat his own corn dogs because he had only three teeth left—two on the bottom and one on the top.

"Corn dogs, corn dogs! Git yer yellow mustard and corn dogs!" he bellowed like an auctioneer.

He wore a dingy black-and-white striped railroad conductor's cap. Word had it that Cappy used to be an old steam engine captain in New Mexico. Or maybe he just made it up to sell corn dogs. Either way, the shtick worked.

"Why does he shout like he's getting punched in the stomach?" Gabriel asked his mother as they waited in a long line.

"He's trying to get customers," Maggie said through a chuckle.

"Looks like he has plenty of those. Look how long the line is."

Maggie smiled contentedly, grateful for a good day, appreciative that they were making a happy memory. Holding hands and swinging them like two kids, they waited in line with Miss Vonda for their very own Cappy corn dog.

Gabriel dug into his corn dog fiercely, occasionally splattering yellow mustard on his shirt, but he didn't care. The two contentedly strolled past the vendors and their wares.

Miss Vonda finished off the last bite of corn dog. "Earl must be buying a lot more vegetables for him to be gone this long," she said.

"Oh, look at these beautiful handbags," Maggie said with a longing in her voice. She didn't have the money for such luxuries, but she loved to browse. "Look at the stitching. And the leather is so soft." She ran her hand over one of the bags.

"That there is gen-yew-ine deer hide. Killed, cleaned, and crafted by yours truly," said the man in the booth.

Maggie didn't dare ask how much. She was just admiring

the beauty of the handbag.

"Gabriel, someday when you have lots of money, you can buy your momma one of these," Maggie said to Gabriel with a grin. Except he wasn't there. She spun her head back around, looking for her son.

"Gabriel," she said loudly.

"Gabriel!" This time she shouted.

"I didn't see him leave," said Miss Vonda.

Her heart sank as she looked in every direction. Mild panic set in as she kept calling his name loudly, but he was nowhere in sight. Miss Vonda turned and walked quickly to the next row of buildings. She stood at a four-way intersection to see if she could find Gabriel. Maggie did the same one row over.

"Gabriel . . . Gabriel Clarke!" Maggie stood on her tippy-toes and peered over the crowd down to the last row—and there he was, about twenty-five yards down the way. He was standing mesmerized in front of a booth.

"I found him!" Maggie yelled to Miss Vonda as she walked furiously toward him. She picked up the pace to a jog, and when she got to him, Maggie grabbed his left arm and spun him around.

"You gotta tell me when you want to go see something! Don't run off like that! You're gonna give your momma a heart attack!"

Gabriel didn't respond. He just looked at her, smiled, and pointed. At the top of the booth, hanging crooked by one nail, was an old-fashioned, hand-carved sign made out of a piece of driftwood that read "Magic River Marbles."

Maggie had never seen this booth, although they had visited the market many times. The fifteen-by-fifteen booth was fronted by a trough made from rough-hewn wood. Inside the trough was crystal clear water, about eight inches deep. The sunlight hit the water in an intriguing way, making it look as if it were actually moving. Maggie could see the reflection of hundreds of beautiful marbles scattered among a bed of smooth grey river stones throughout the trough.

"They look like stars," Gabriel said with wonder in his voice as he peered down into the water.

"Twenty-five cents a handful, and that includes a pouch." A kind and wise voice emanated from behind the trough. A large man with a long, flowing white beard and locks and donning well-worn denim overalls made his way to a rocking chair. He lowered himself slowly and fell back with a sigh. Then he propped his feet up on a wooden crate and rested his right hand over the side of the trough. He twirled the water with his fingers and motioned to Gabriel, who was staring into the water.

"Go ahead, young man. Pick up some marbles. See what you think."

Gabriel immediately reached down and ran his hands through the watery channel. He desperately wanted to select just the right ones. He pulled out three large Aggies. The marbles were clear with beautiful streaks of blue and grey. Gabriel took one between his left thumb and forefinger. Squinting with one eye, he lifted the marble to the light as if looking through a gun scope.

"Those are magic marbles, boy. If you look close, you'll see . . . they have The River in them. Yeah, The River gives the marbles their beauty. "

The old man motioned to Gabriel to hand him an Aggie, which he held into the light.

"Legend has it if you put these type of marbles under your bed while you sleep and think real hard on the good things, they'll give you wonderful dreams."

He handed the Aggie back to Gabriel. He put his feet down, leaned forward, and raised his eyebrows. With a little mystery in his voice he declared, "I'm talking about dreams where you'll have the courage to follow your heart, and nothing will stop you. The River is alive, you know. It never stops moving. Every time you look at each marble, you'll see something you haven't seen before. That's the magic of The River in there."

Maggie looked down at Gabriel.

Without moving, still staring at the marble, Gabriel said, "Mom, can I? Can I buy some marbles?"

Without hesitation, Maggie reached into the pocket of her skirt and pulled out a handful of coins.

"Here, Gabe," she said as she lowered her hand and offered it to Gabriel.

With wet fingers, he picked out the only quarter in the handful of coins and immediately passed it to the old man, who handed him a leather pouch about the size of a baseball.

"Fill it up, young man . . . as many as you can stuff in there."

Gabriel dropped in the three Aggies and then took his

time examining several marbles in the trough. One by one, he dipped his hand into the water and dropped them into his pouch. He stuffed his pouch so full that he could barely close the drawstring.

"It was a pleasure doing business with you, son. I hope you enjoy them." The old man gazed at the boy with a generous smile on his face.

"What do you say, Gabriel?" his mother asked.

Gabriel finally took his eyes off of the marbles, looked up at the kind man, and said, "Thank you."

The old man chuckled like Santa Claus.

"All the best, young man. All the best."

Gabriel and Maggie, along with Miss Vonda, headed back toward the lemonade stand, where they met up with Mister Earl. They made their way back to the pick-up truck to start the journey home. Gabriel jumped in the back right away. He sat down, put his legs together, and began taking his marbles out one at a time to look at them and count them.

"You better put them back in the pouch while we drive," his mother said before she got in the truck.

After they pulled out of the parking lot, Miss Vonda made an observation. "When that boy sees something he wants, he just goes after it, doesn't he? My goodness, though. What a scare that was when we couldn't find him."

Maggie didn't reply as she stared out the window in a daze. Memories of life at The River—life with John—came flooding back. She remembered how much she used to love living near The River. There was a freshness in the air and an adventure to life when they were together at Corley Falls. But that was six years ago. She hadn't been around The River since Gabriel was two. After a few minutes passed, Miss Vonda spoke up again.

"You okay, dear?"

"Oh . . . uh . . . yeah, I'm okay."

"Was it just the marbles? That boy is crazy about marbles."

Maggie paused for a second, then looked at Miss Vonda with a thoughtful smile.

"His daddy used to play marbles with him. I think it's more than just the marbles, but I don't know. It was a good day, Miss Vonda . . . a good day."

The next time they went to the All County Farmer's Market, Maggie and Gabriel searched for the person they called The River Marble Man. He was nowhere to be found.

They dropped by the main office to ask for the whereabouts of the old man with a white beard and white hair who sold marbles sitting at the bottom of a water-filled trough.

The manager said he didn't know whom they were talking about, nor could he find a record of a man going by that description.

"Sounds like a mystery to me," said the man in charge. "Apparently, he was just passing through town."

CHAPTER 5

MISTER EARL AND THE PIG TRIP

The first days of spring in Cairo were beautiful. The warm air and steady breeze across the plains coaxed millions of wildflowers to erupt everywhere. Like the arrival of a letter from a best friend, the longer days of spring opened with anticipation and the encouragement of a fresh start.

The last few years had been fairly uneventful for Gabriel. He was managing well in school, and the "hard days" were fewer now, but they still came from time to time. As his confidence grew, however, so did his impetuous nature. The few freckles on his cheeks were more pronounced, and his hair had turned darker.

His frame was certainly lengthening. At age eleven, he was just a few inches shy of his mom's five-foot, six-inch stature. He was unusually strong for his age, and Mister Earl liked to utilize his help around the farm from time to time. He could manage most of the tools now, and splitting logs was one of his favorites. He liked how strong he felt when he drove the axe right through the wood with one giant swing.

Then again, nothing beat driving the tractor, but that was a rare treat.

———————

It was the end of a hard week for Maggie. She was concerned about her son, who was approaching the difficult adolescent years without a father to guide him through. She awoke every day with that thought occupying the back of her mind.

The diner was slow, which cut into her tips. One Friday, she arrived home at 3:30 from her early shift. Walking slowly up the front porch steps, she opened the rickety screen door and dropped her keys and purse on the farm table in the kitchen.

"I'm home," she announced. "Hello . . . anybody here?" She walked over to the pull-handle icebox and yanked on the handle like it was a slot machine.

"Okay. I'm going to eat this last piece of cherry pie," she said, raising the pitch of her voice. The house was eerily quiet except for the tinkling of the wind chimes that Mister Earl had hung outside the kitchen window.

She lit the gas stove and filled her teapot with water before she sat down at the table. Slouching in her chair, she let out a big sigh and stared at the small piece of pie, trying to find comfort in its presence.

"I guess it's just you and me," she muttered.

She got up and took off her work apron and hung it on a hook by the clock. While she waited for her water to boil, she decided to change out of her work clothes, which smelled like a combination of bacon grease and stale coffee. As she began to take the bobby pins out of her hair, she rounded the corner into the bedroom and was immediately startled.

"Oh, Gabriel, you scared me! I didn't think anyone was home," she gasped with both hands over her chest.

Gabriel didn't look up. He was sitting on his cot with his legs crossed, staring at the floor. There, in his lap, was a picture.

"Gabe? Honey?" Maggie walked closer to him and saw the picture—a black-and-white photograph yellowed with age. It was a snapshot of his father, John Clarke, holding Gabriel when he was four years old. The tow-headed boy had his right arm around the back of his dad's neck, and the other one was pointing at the camera.

Both of them had spectacular smiles on their faces. They were standing in front of The River at Big Water Camp on the day before the big hike and the tragedy that would change their lives forever.

Maggie's eyes immediately welled up as she cupped her left hand over her quivering mouth. She tried to hold tears back, but she couldn't. The scene of her little boy staring at a picture she hadn't seen in years took her off guard.

She paused for a moment to collect herself.

"Oh, sweetheart." She sat down on the cot next to him, put her arm around his shoulder, and pulled him in close. Gabriel sniffled.

"That's a great picture. Look at those crystal eyes of yours."

Gabriel did not respond. He pulled his right hand up and wiped eyes with one aggressive stroke.

"Look how small you were . . . your blond hair . . . ."

Gabriel interrupted her without looking up.

"You weren't there. Why weren't you there?" Gabriel asked with a firm tone.

"What, honey?" Maggie was taken back by the question.

"Why did The River take my dad? Why?" Gabriel's voice was getting louder. "I want my dad! The River didn't need my father. I was on the mountain, and you weren't there. I waited for Dad, and he never came back. The River took him, and you weren't there." Gabriel began to sob uncontrollably. He picked up the picture and turned it toward Maggie. "I want him back! I want him back!" Maggie didn't know what to do.

"I know, honey. I know. I'm sorry." She had always felt so much guilt and remorse that she had left for Kansas just weeks before the accident.

Gabriel stuffed the picture into his pocket and stormed out of the bedroom onto the front porch. Mister Earl was on his way in from the fields when he bumped into Gabriel on the front porch stairs. He watched the boy storm past him and run off toward the barn.

"Gabriel!" Maggie shouted in desperation from the front porch.

Mister Earl looked down and fidgeted with his keys in his pocket.

"I'll go check on him," he said solemnly.

Maggie nodded and choked back more tears.

Mister Earl walked outside and slowly made his way into the barn. He didn't see the boy at first, but further in he saw Gabriel sitting with his back against the large rear tractor tire.

"You think you can help me with something tomorrow?" Mister Earl asked.

Gabriel was drawing in the sawdust floor with his finger.

Mister Earl shuffled his feet. "I'm going to the pig sale tomorrow. I could use a hand with those rascals. Then maybe I'll take you to my favorite thing in the world."

That last statement caught Gabriel's attention. He looked up with swollen eyes at the older gentleman.

"You can't go with me to my favorite thing unless you help me get rid of some of those pigs though."

"I'll help," Gabriel said with curiosity in his voice.

"We leave at daybreak." Mister Earl turned and started to walk out of the barn.

"Uh . . . what's your favorite thing?"

"You'll find out tomorrow."

———◆◆◆———

Gabriel woke up the next morning just before daylight. He was excited to be going with Mister Earl. The boy soaked up any attention he got from the man. Gabriel ran out to the barnyard and found Mister Earl slapping the pigs on the rump.

"Yaw, pig, yaw . . . get in there," he bellowed as he rustled several pigs up the ramp into the back of the truck. He could fit about seven fattened hogs into the truck bed. Gabriel stood on the bottom rung of the fence and watched.

"Gabriel, go get that last one, would ya? He ain't co-operating today."

"Isn't that Sinus?" Every now and then, Mister Earl would name a pig if it had some kind of distinctive trait. Sinus had an eternal runny snout.

Mister Earl tramped over into the barn. Gabriel jumped over the fence and inched his way over to the last behemoth trying to avoid becoming bacon.

"Come on, Sinus! Yaw pig!" Gabriel yelled. The pig let out a snort and sprinted up into the truck bed, which had wooden fence sides to keep the pigs inside.

"That was easy!" Thrilled with his accomplishment, Gabriel closed the rear gate. Mister Earl came back from the barn carrying a couple of fishing poles and a mesh bag.

"Is that your favorite thing?" he asked enthusiastically.

"Yep. Now go get that cooler on the front seat and go get some ice. We gotta keep these chicken livers cold, or they will stink us up good and Miss Vonda won't let me back in the house. Catfish love chicken livers."

"Fishing!" Gabriel was thrilled and nervous all at once. He'd always wanted to go fishing. His friends at The Pond asked him to fish from time to time, but because of his fear of water, he would always find something else to do. Mister Earl would keep him safe, though.

After a ninety-minute ride, they arrived at the auction barn. People from all over showed up every third Saturday to sell their swine.

"These pigs look fat this time," Mister Earl said as they parked. "Here's hoping they weigh good and heavy. Some extra money would come in handy to fix the back fence at the farm."

The auction went very well. They sold their seven hogs within an hour and a half and made their way back to the truck. Gabriel noticed that Mister Earl had more pep in his walk now. The pigs weighed in quite heavy, and now he had the extra cash he needed to do necessary repairs around the farm.

The pig sale took place close to the Kansas and Oklahoma border. They got into the truck and headed south for another half hour. They turned off the main roads and onto a curvy dirt road that led them into wooded terrain. Mister Earl slowed down and made the last hairpin turn to the right before the woods opened up to a beautiful bluff.

About one hundred yards ahead was the Arkansas River, which made a slow bending turn. With a steady, firm current, the ripples in the river reflected the sun's rays like a million flickering candles. Massive cottonwood trees lined each bank like mighty soldiers on guard.

"Not many people know about this spot. That's why I like it."

He pulled the truck underneath a shady area about fifty yards from the water. All they could hear was the lapping of gentle rapids and the sound of the leafy trees applauding softly as the warm breeze would come and go. Mister Earl started to untie the poles. Gabriel didn't move. He was transfixed by the broad and majestic river.

"Gabriel, can you grab the cooler and this bucket back here?"

Gabriel opened his door slowly, still staring at the water.

"That's a big river, Mister Earl," he said cautiously.

"Yep. She's big, and she's got lots of catfish in her right now. Let's go catch us some dinner." Mister Earl walked on ahead, carrying the fishing poles. Gabriel had the cooler and an empty five-gallon paint bucket to put the fish in.

Gabriel felt himself getting nervous as they got closer to the water. His heart beat faster. He'd carried a healthy fear of lakes and rivers since his father's accident. The episode at The Pond only made it worse. He didn't think that fishing meant he would have to get close to the river.

Mister Earl got his pole and started baiting his hook. "You gotta work the hook through the chicken liver two or three times to make sure it's on there good. Watch yourself on the hook. Once it gets in you, it dudn't want to come out."

Gabriel watched Mister Earl put on waders. "Are you going in the water?"

"Sure," the old man replied. "That's where the fish are, aren't they?"

"I think I'll just watch for now." Gabriel said.

"Suit yourself."

Gabriel turned the bucket over and sat down. All he could think about was how big the river was and how much he didn't want to go into the water.

Mister Earl slogged out in his waders, and once the water got up to his knees, he cast a line baited with a chicken liver upstream. The bait splashed into the water, and he waited for the line to slowly pass him and head downstream. In an instant, though, his rod bent violently, and he yanked it up, setting the hook on the fish.

"Yee-hooo, fish!" he yelled as he cranked the reel. It took him only about fifteen seconds to reel his first catfish to the surface.

"Boy, those things fight!" Mister Earl reached into the water and grabbed the fish, placing his thumb into its the mouth and his fingers into the gills. The catfish must have been two feet long or better, and a plump one at that. Mister Earl hoisted the flapping fish and walked toward Gabriel.

"See? He's smilin' at ya!"

Gabriel was surprised. Mister Earl wasn't usually this talkative—or happy, for that matter. Gabriel, grinning from ear to ear, stood up to greet him.

"Fill up that bucket with some water, Gabe. We got us some fish here!"

Gabriel did as he was told, and Mister Earl dumped his first fish into the paint bucket. He waded back out into the river, and lo and behold, he got another strike right away. This kept happening over and over until the fish bucket was nearly full.

Gabriel loved watching Mister Earl fish, and he was feeling more at ease by the river. He took off his shoes and began sticking his toes in just off the bank.

"Hey, Mister Earl . . . Mister Earl!" He had to shout since a breeze had picked up and Mister Earl had waded upstream a little further. "Can I catch one?"

Mister Earl reeled in his line and sloshed back to shore. As he got closer, he held up an empty hook at the end of his line.

"You see that? There's a thief out there stealing my bait. Let's get you fixed up. Then I'll take you out there."

"I don't want to go too far out."

"We won't. But if you want to catch a fish, you gotta get out a little ways to reach 'em."

Mister Earl returned to the truck, where he fetched a second pair of waders from behind the front seat.

"These are Miss Vonda's. They'll be a little big for ya, but they'll do. Lord knows I can't get her to wear 'em."

Gabriel slipped on the rubber waders and listened as Mister Earl showed him again how to put a chicken liver on the hook. Then he waded out slowly with Mister Earl, who was pushing forward very methodically. At knee-deep level, Gabriel could feel the easy current pushing his waders against the left side of his legs.

"Okay, that's good," Mister Earl said. "That's far enough."

Gabriel knew it was a big deal that he was even in the water, but he felt safe with Mister Earl.

"Before you cast, what you wanna do is look behind you to make sure no one is there, or any trees for that matter. Then bring your rod back nice and easy and toss the tip forward. Then release the line at the end."

Mister Earl took Gabriel's pole and cast the line out, then reeled it back in. "There . . . you try."

He handed the rod to Gabriel and moved to give him room. Gabriel brought the rod back over his right shoulder and launched his arm forward. The rod and reel flew out of his hand and splashed in the river.

"Oh, no!" Gabriel couldn't believe what happened.

"Aw, geez," Mister Earl exclaimed. He hustled after the rod and reel and snatched it before the river took it downstream.

"I'm sorry. I don't know what happened," Gabriel said.

"I do. You let go of it! But at least it was a cork rod, so it floated." Mister Earl was chuckling now.

It only took Gabriel a couple more tries before he got the hang of the casting. On his fifth cast, he was watching as the bobber and bait floated downstream, and in an instant, the tip of his rod got bent over and yanked into the water.

"Pull up! Pull up!" Mister Earl yelled. "Crank him in hard. You got a giant on the line!"

Gabriel obeyed, even though it was difficult because the rod jerked violently. It took him several minutes, but he reeled the catfish in, which Mister Earl grabbed.

"That thing is every bit of twenty pounds!"

Gabriel jumped up and down, laughing. His hands and legs splashed about. He had never felt such joy.

"Wait until Mom sees this!"

"This right here is why it's my favorite thing." Mister Earl regarded the catfish with a smile as wide as Texas.

———◆———

They fished another hour before packing up to head home. They were tired from the dawn departure and the adventures of the day. With his right elbow perched on the passenger door, and his eyes squinting from the setting sunshine, Gabriel was considering the memories he had made.

"I didn't know The River was like that."

"Like what?"

"I don't know. The River wasn't so scary. It was calm and stuff. I liked it. I wanna go again."

"I think The River liked you too," Mister Earl said with his hand resting on the wheel. "The River has a way, you know. It reminds me of what's important. That's why I like to go."

"Well, The River gave us dinner," Gabriel said with a precocious grin, looking over to Mister Earl.

"That it did, young man. That it did."

Warm air rushed through the open passenger window, and the sound of the rumbling engine and the tires against the road were all Gabriel needed to lean his head back and drift off to sleep for the rest of the way home.

It had been a good day.

ᴄꜱ THE NEW TEACHER ᴃᴄ

Starting a new school year was never one of Gabriel's favorite things. The first school day on the Tuesday after Labor Day meant meeting new kids who might not be nice, getting used to a new teacher who might be too strict, and studying every night, which was just plain hard work for him.

Sixth grade, Gabriel decided on the first day of school, would be pure evil. He'd rather do anything else than listen to a boring teacher or those stuck-up girls who played "teacher's pet" in the classroom but were so mean on the schoolyard.

Last year, Gabriel had to sit next to Thelma Lou Nichols. She wore thick round spectacles, thick as magnifying glasses, scratched the back of her head constantly, and smelled like a giant mothball. She never stopped talking and commenting about everything. And she was the worst tetherball player in the class.

Gabriel loved playing tetherball and kickball at recess time, and the start of his sixth grade year was no different. But two weeks in, an unexpected event happened that would affect Gabriel forever.

It was a Monday morning, and all fourteen students scrambled to their seats as the school bell rang. His teacher, Mrs. Jewel, always made her students write extra sentences if they were late for school.

J.J. Hopper, self-nicknamed "The General," sauntered in after the bell as if he owned the place.

"You're gonna get sentences, J.J.," Naomi Ledbetter said smugly from her front row chair.

But Mrs. Jewel was nowhere to be seen, which almost never happened. She had been teaching elementary school for over forty-five years. At the age of seventy-four, she still had a lot of energy. She didn't put up with much guff from the boys, but she could be funny on occasion. At five feet, four inches, Mrs. Jewel had rosy cheeks and dirty white hair pulled up in a stacked bun atop her head. She wore handmade farm dresses, and in the fall and spring months, she put a flower from her garden in her hair. She never wore makeup and always smelled like baby powder and cinnamon rolls.

Gabriel's classmates, who started chattering about the exploits of the weekend, quickly got quiet when Mr. Van Buren, the school principal, walked into the classroom. Gabriel saw him only at school assemblies *or* if he was in serious trouble.

"Good morning, class," he began. "I have some bad news. I got a call over the weekend from Mrs. Jewel's husband, Frank.

Frank told me she has fallen ill and will not be able to continue teaching you, at least for the time being. She will be okay, but she needs to work on getting better. The doctor has ordered complete bed rest, so it seems she will be out for a while."

Mr. Van Buren held up a large piece of folded construction paper in his right hand.

"She wrote all of you a card that I will leave up here on the desk for you to read at the appropriate time."

The kids sat quietly, stunned by the news.

"Now I'd like to introduce you to your substitute teacher. I expect you to give her the same respect you gave Mrs. Jewel."

On cue, a figure walked into the classroom quietly.

"Ah . . . here she is. Class, I'd like you to meet Miss Lily Collingsworth." He motioned to her with his right hand. "Well, don't just sit there, say hello!"

"Hello, Miss Collingsworth," the class muttered in a broken unison.

"Hello, everyone," she said softly with an inviting smile. Gabriel and his classmates couldn't take their eyes off of her. She didn't look like anyone else in Cairo.

Miss Collingsworth was tall and thin with a rich mocha skin coloring. With a flawless complexion, her hair was jet black, long and shiny—pouring down her head to the small of her back like a dark waterfall. Her eyes were black as coal, full of mystery and warmth at the same time.

She began to walk up and down the rows of desks, taking her time to ask each student his or her name. They all turned in their seats and followed her every move.

She returned to the front of the classroom. "I am so excited to be teaching you this year," she said. "We are going to learn so much together."

She looked around and made eye contact with several students, including Gabriel. "Learning is about exploration and fun. Learning is at the base of everything in life. No matter how old you are, you never stop learning. Every time you learn something new, it's like discovering a treasure."

She rested her hand on a globe standing at the side of her desk. "We are going to learn about other parts of our world, explore the way other people live and their history, and go on field trips. You'll also hear me tell stories. Oh, I love good stories."

Miss Collingsworth spoke so passionately that even J.J. was listening. She continued talking as she walked among the seated students. When she passed by Gabriel, who sat third from the back on the right hand side of the room, she moved the air as she glided by. Gabriel couldn't help but notice that she smelled like fresh mint.

She clapped her hands. "I have an idea. Let's all get up and push our chairs to the outside of the room."

The students didn't make a move.

"Come on, it's okay. It will be nice."

Slowly, one by one, the students started to slide their desks to the perimeter of the room—although J.J. used the opportunity to play bumper cars.

"Okay, settle down, guys. Let's sit down in a circle."

She hunched on her knees and sat down on the floor, which

the students did as well. Gabriel made sure he was directly across from her so she could see him.

J.J. piped up. "We are not going to have to sing, are we?"

Miss Collingsworth laughed. "You don't sing, J.J.? Aw, come on. I bet you have a pretty voice." All the boys laughed, and the girls giggled.

"J.J.'s got a pretty voice! J.J.'s got a pretty voice!" teased one boy.

"Shut up!" J.J. said, making a fist.

Miss Collingsworth quickly redirected them. "Okay, everyone. I've *heard* your names, but I need to learn them. Why don't we go around the room and you say your name again and . . . tell us what your favorite food is. I'll start. I'm Lily Collingsworth, and my favorite food is definitely chocolate."

The kids went around the circle, and one at a time recited their names. Most of the favorite foods were some kind of candy or ice cream flavor. Gabriel got a little nervous when it was his turn. He was having a hard time deciding what his favorite food was.

"Well, uh, it's either Miss Vonda's biscuits or Cappy's corn dogs at the All County Farmer's Market."

J.J., the General, sat next to Gabriel.

"Hear, hear! To pick a favorite is too difficult for me. *All* food is your friend!" J.J. declared. He reached over and patted Gabriel on the back so hard that others could hear the thump, and then he grabbed his soft belly with both hands and wiggled it back and forth. Everyone broke into laughter.

After they made their way around the room, Miss

Collingsworth took over again.

"I want you all to know that I'm looking forward to getting to know each and every one of you. We'll have a great year. Now, do you have any questions for me?"

Several hands shot up in the air. Questions like:

"Are we going to have lots of homework?"

"Can we have extra-long recess on Fridays?"

"How many books are we going to have to read?"

Then Naomi Ledbetter, the prissy blonde-haired, blue-eyed girl with nothing ever out of place, spoke up and shocked everyone with her question.

"Why are you so dark-skinned?"

The class froze and waited for the teacher's response. Miss Collingsworth raised her eyebrows and didn't miss a beat.

"I'm glad you asked, Naomi. Just like you, I am unique. Did you know that no two people on the planet are exactly alike? There never has been or ever will be another person created exactly like you. You are one of a kind . . . and so am I. Everyone is unique and made for a specific purpose. We all have an individual path to follow. I am thankful for my brown skin. It reminds me of my history, where I come from. I am a descendant of the Cherokee Indian people."

The children were dead silent and spellbound by her words. Their new teacher stood up and approached the blackboard, where she wrote in big letters: AYKWA-AYKWANEE.

"Can anyone pronounce this?" She pointed to the board with her long elegant fingers. All of the children tried to sound out the letters simultaneously.

"Okay, okay, not too bad," she said with a smile. "It's actually not too hard to say. Everyone say 'ay.' "

"Ay," they all repeated.

"Now 'kwah.' "

"Kwah!" they said in a louder voice.

"Now say it together, 'Ay-kwah.' "

"Ay-kwah," they repeated.

"Good! Now just add 'knee,' like the knee of your leg."

After a "knee" chorus, she said, "Now say 'Ay-kwah-knee . . . good . . . now Ay-kwah ay-kwah-knee.' Got it?"

The students repeated the phrase several times together until they were able to say it correctly.

"You have to say it with rhythm," Miss Collingsworth said. "The Cherokee language is rhythmic and has motion to it. It is the rhythm of the earth."

"What does it mean?" Naomi asked.

"Aykwa-Aykwanee is my Cherokee name. Do you want to know what it means?"

"Yes!" they all responded.

"Aykwa-Aykwanee means Great River."

The new teacher transfixed Gabriel. His mouth hung open as he watched her speak. He thought about how much he liked the sound of her voice and how she was so kind. Miss Collingsworth wasn't like anyone he had ever known. And now he would get to spend the whole school year with her.

Gabriel was startled out of his reverie when Miss Collingsworth directed a question to him. "Gabriel, have you ever seen a beautiful river?"

He had trouble mustering a response so Miss Collingsworth continued her talk. "I grew up in a small town in the beautiful mountains of North Carolina," she said. "Has anyone ever been to North Carolina?"

Several hands shot up in the room. Miss Collingsworth called on Dickie Colter, Gabriel's nemesis.

"Gabriel is scared of The Pond. He's scared of everything," he said. "He probably wouldn't even get near a river!"

Gabriel hung his head at his classmate's berating tone.

Miss Collingsworth came to his defense. "I think we all have some fears we have to deal with. Let's focus on saying kind things, okay?"

Gabriel was thankful his new teacher took up for him. He relaxed in his chair as Miss Collingsworth picked up where she had left off.

"We lived near a beautiful river in North Carolina called the Nantahala. The Nantahala is a strong and powerful river with thunderous and powerful sections where the water crashes down through the mountains and creates beautiful whitewater foam. The Nantahala also has tranquil and serene sections. There are places where the river is *so* calm that it acts like a perfect mirror to reflect the mountains and trees around it.

"I love the river so much. My grandfather used to take our family to a special place on the river to make a fire, sing songs, and enjoy a cookout. We always sat next to a beautiful waterfall. One day I, along with my three brothers and mother, were there with my grandfather. I was only four years old at the time. We were sitting around the campfire, and my grandfather began to speak. He didn't talk very much so when he spoke, we listened. He said, 'The River brings life to everything in the canyon. The waters of this Great River washed over Aykwa-Aykwanee and gave her beautiful skin—the color of the earth.' He pointed to me that night and said, 'You bring us life and love, Little River. Full of thunder and full of beauty.' Everyone laughed because I was so small, but I had a strong will." She raised her fists as if to flex her arms.

The children sat captivated by her story. Gabriel was in awe of every word. If angels were real, she just might be one. An American Indian angel, sent to Cairo elementary just for him.

"Where was your father?" The intuitive question came from Stephen J. Fremont. A normally quiet kid, Gabriel knew him to be a genuinely curious person.

"He couldn't be there that day because he was no longer with us," she said as her countenance dropped.

"Where was he?" Stephen said.

"He went to the great sky. That's what we call heaven. Yeah, he died. I still miss him very much."

Gabriel connected to her grief in a profound way. She, too, had lost her father, just like him. Maybe she understood how he felt. Maybe she had the bad dreams, too.

After a wonderful day getting to know his new teacher, the obnoxious school bell rang, signifying their freedom. Like ants under a magnifying glass, the students scrambled out of the classroom, except for one. Gabriel took his time gathering his things before approaching her desk.

Miss Collingsworth looked up from the sheet of paper she

was reading. "Do you need any help with anything?"

Gabriel stood there awkwardly. "Do you think I could show you my marble collection sometime? I have hundreds of them. I've also gone fishing with Mister Earl at The River. It's his favorite thing to do. I could show you how to play marbles. I'm really good."

Gabriel didn't come up for air because he was excited to talk to Miss Collingsworth.

"That would be nice, Gabriel." She set her folder down. "Which do you like better, marbles or fishing?"

Gabriel thought for a minute. "Well, I've been fishing only once, but I loved it. But I also love marbles because my dad loved marbles, and we played them when we were together."

"The great thing is that you can love doing both things." Miss Collingsworth smiled. "I'd love to see your marble collection sometime. And try not to let what Dickie said get to you. Kids who lash out like that are probably very sad or hurt for some reason, so they take it out on other kids."

"Thank you, Miss Collingsworth. Goodbye." Gabriel started toward the door.

"See you tomorrow, Gabriel."

Gabriel paused at the door.

"Yes?"

"My dad died, too. He grew up near The River. He loved it. I'll tell you about him sometime."

"I would like that very much."

Gabriel turned and walked out, thankful for a new friend in Miss Collingsworth.

CHAPTER 7

A Visitor Comes to the Farm

On a bitterly cold Saturday morning in the last week of February in 1963, four inches of snow still covered the ground from a storm that passed through Kansas a week earlier. The farm was covered in a beautiful white blanket—crisp and quiet—as far as the eye could see. A deer in the field gingerly poked its hooves through the frozen layers, looking for something to munch on.

"Move, Fi Fi! Get out of my way, or I'm going to make you dinner."

Gabriel scolded the hen—repeating what he heard Mister Earl say from time to time—as he cleaned the coop. Like with the pigs, naming the animals was a form of entertainment while performing otherwise monotonous chores. Mister Earl used to say, "That big fat hen looks like she thinks she is better than all the others." The name Fi Fi seemed to fit.

Bundled with a thick wool coat, knit gloves, and toboggan hat, Gabriel could see the steam from his breath as he raked the pen. Miss Vonda was in the kitchen, cleaning up after one of her Saturday morning pancake feasts. Mister Earl was in the old barn, straightening his tools and scraping mud and ice off of the tractor. His mother was working at the diner, something she did every other Saturday. She didn't mind since Saturday mornings were usually a good time for tips. His mom said that everyone seemed happier on the weekends, so they were a little more generous.

"You know what tomorrow is, don't you?" Gabriel liked talking to the animals while he did his chores; they kept him company. He continued talking while the hens clucked around the coop.

Although the chickens may not have been too excited, Gabriel was thrilled to tell them about what would happen the next day: on Sunday, February 24, he would turn twelve years old. He figured that being one year away from becoming an official teenager would mean at least one special present because his mom always made him feel that his birthday was the Most Important Day of the Year.

Maybe Miss Vonda will make me my favorite dinner . . . fried chicken!

The chickens clucked, as if they understood they could end up in the fryer. Gabriel finished his cleaning, shut the coop door, and made his way over to the barn to put the bucket and rake away. Then he heard the sound of Mister Earl knocking the ice off the back of the tractor.

"I'm done with the coop," Gabriel announced.

No reply.

"You know what tomorrow is, right, Mister Earl?"

Mister Earl peeked around the large back tire of the tractor. "Yep . . . it's Sunday."

Gabriel let out a sigh.

"Do you know what else it is?"

"Yep . . . the twenty-fourth of February."

Gabriel hung the rake up on the wall with other tools and walked around the back of the tractor. "It's more than that! Don't you remember?"

"Oh yeah, it's the day we're supposed to finish repainting the front porch rocking chairs."

"Aw, come on, Mister Earl. It's my birthday!"

Mister Earl was chuckling now.

"Oh, yeah, that's right." A sheepish grin came across his grizzled face. "You're going to be ten, right?"

"Twelve!" Gabriel said emphatically.

"Well. You have only sixty-two more years to catch me."

"What did you do on your twelfth birthday?"

"Oh, gosh, I don't think I can remember that far back. I was probably working. I can't recall a time when I didn't work. Maybe my folks let me go fishing. That's all I really cared about back then." Mister Earl kept chipping away at the ice.

"Can we go fishing again sometime? I really liked that a lot."

"We'll go fishing again when spring comes." Mister Earl continued concentrating on the tractor.

"You should grab an armload of wood for the house. The

fire probably needs to be stoked."

Another chore. Gabriel walked over to the far side of the barn, where he lifted the tarp off of a large stack of split wood. He filled his arms with as much wood as he could carry and started trekking toward the house, grateful he could thaw out a bit inside the heated home. He dropped the wood in a stack by the cast iron potbelly stove in the living room, took off his coat and hat, and hung them on the coat rack. He opened the hinged door and dropped another two more logs on the fire. Then he stepped back onto the front porch and retreated to their tiny apartment attached to the back of house.

The sound of a vehicle coming, crunching up the long frozen drive, broke the stillness of the morning.

Who would be coming to the farm at ten a.m. on a Saturday? Mom doesn't usually get home until after lunch.

Gabriel ran over to the window and pulled the curtain back. A faded black Ford step-side pick-up was coming up the long driveway. He couldn't quite see who was behind the wheel, but when the truck parked to the side of the house, he saw the driver door open and his teacher, Miss Collingsworth, step out.

Gabriel's heart thumped as the schoolteacher gracefully shut her door and walked around to the passenger side of her truck with hands jammed inside her coat pockets against the cold. She was wearing a three-quarter length, thick brown suede jacket with a red knit cap pulled down over her ears. Her long black braids flowed over her shoulders, and her brown cheeks were as smooth as ever.

Am I in trouble? he wondered. *Why is she here?*

He quickly did an inventory in his head of the past week of school. He had handed in all his homework. He was ready for her famous pop quizzes.

She opened the passenger side door and pulled out a flat package wrapped in brown paper. Gabriel quickly closed the curtains and reached for a book that was required reading during the semester. That would impress her.

———————◆◆◆———————

Miss Collingsworth came up to the front door of the main house and rang the tiny dinner bell that hung on the porch. Miss Vonda dried her hands at the sink and went over to open the door.

"Hi there, I'm Lily Collingsworth, Gabriel's teacher. I'm at the right address, aren't I?"

"Yes, dear. Their room is around back, but come on in. I can let Gabriel know you're here," Miss Vonda said with a coy grin. "Would you let me fix you some tea before I go get him?"

"That would be wonderful. It's so cold out. May I set this down over here?"

"Of course, wherever you like." Miss Vonda left to boil water on the stove.

Miss Collingsworth followed her into the kitchen, where they conversed nonstop for the next half hour over their cup of tea.

———————◆◆◆———————

Through the thin walls, Gabriel overheard them discussing their favorite foods, the hairdressers in Cairo—there were only two of them—and, of course, the fact that tomorrow was his birthday. So far, there was no sign of him being in trouble at school.

"Well, I brought Gabriel something for his birthday," Miss Collingsworth said. "He's one of those students who really captured my heart from the beginning. I love all my students and I love teaching, but there's just something about that boy. I suppose I see a little of myself in him. Anyway, I have something for him."

Gabriel couldn't believe his ears. The affirmation and care in her voice were so comforting. He had never had someone go out of the way like this to show him love. Gabriel left his bedroom, came around to the front of the house, and poked his head into the kitchen.

"Hey, Gabriel!" Miss Collingsworth stood up and opened her arms.

"Hi," he said sheepishly as he accepted her hug.

"I have something for you." She walked next to the front door and picked up a package and handed it to him. "I know I'm a day early, but . . . Happy Birthday!"

Gabriel took the present into his hands and held it with a huge smile.

"Well, go ahead and open it. I think you'll like what's inside," she remarked with anticipation.

Gabriel sat down on the sofa and placed the package on his lap. The present was two or three feet wide and lay flat across his legs. He untied the red bow and tore into the golden paper.

"Look at this!" Gabriel held up a stunning oil landscape painting.

"That's where I grew up," Miss Collingsworth explained. "That's The River that I told you about when we first met. I loved all of the questions you asked me about The River and my experiences there, so I thought you might like my painting."

"You painted it?" Gabriel asked.

"Yes, just for you."

Gabriel, speechless, stared at the beautiful landscape.

Miss Vonda was impressed as well. "My goodness, that's gorgeous. I've never met anyone who could paint like that," she said with both hands on her cheeks.

To Gabriel's eyes, the landscape of The River carving its way through a dramatic gorge had vibrant colors and deep dimension. Gabriel's eyes followed the textures of the brush, which left him with a feeling that he was there, overlooking The River. The details were outstanding: rushing white water over smooth rocks and boulders, tall firs that stretched to the heavens, deer wandering close to the water's edge, and a lonely white bird of prey with a red tail swooping through the air.

Gabriel just ran his hands gently over the dark oak frame and stared at every detail. Hidden in plain sight was a signature in black ink painted in the bottom right-hand corner: Aykwa-Aykwanee.

Miss Collingsworth glanced over at him. "Do you like it?"

Gabriel didn't dare take his eyes away from the painting.

"Yes, ma'am. It's perfect. It's just perfect. Do I get to keep it?"

She laughed. "Of course! Happy Birthday, Gabriel Clarke."

A few minutes later, his teacher reached over and gave Gabriel another hug and stood to put her coat back on. "I better get going. I have to run some errands and get my house cleaned."

Miss Vonda helped her with her coat and walked her out. Gabriel said goodbye, then ran back to the painting to have another look. He was overwhelmed that she would go to this kind of trouble for him. To spend so many hours painting such a beautiful scene just for him was unbelievable.

Whenever Miss Collingsworth was around, he felt like everything would be all right . . . not perfect . . . but all right. He thought about how kind she was and how her breathtaking Indian beauty made her seem like an angel from history past . . . like Pocahontas or Sacagawea. He had read about them in his history lessons.

He had daydreamed about great adventures where Miss Collingsworth was his guide in the wild. Together, they would discover great lands, track wildlife, and follow rivers wherever they would lead. They would make a great team—like Lewis and Clark.

After they finished off ham sandwiches for lunch, Maggie got home from work, bushed from waiting tables at the Cairo Diner.

"Hey, everybody," she announced as she stepped through the front door.

Before she could get any more words out of her mouth, Gabriel piped up.

"Mom, I've got to show you something. Right now. Come on!" He grabbed her hand and tried to lead her to their room around the back of the house.

"Gabriel, honey. I haven't eaten yet, so let me sit down for a minute. I'm tired." Sometimes her son didn't understand what it was like to stand on your feet for seven hours at a time.

"You want a ham sandwich?" asked Miss Vonda.

"That would be great. Thank you so much. The diner was really busy today. I bet I didn't stop moving my entire shift."

Gabriel was getting anxious. "Mom, seriously. You have to come see what I got for my birthday!"

"Someone got you something for your birthday? I thought your birthday wasn't until next week," she said with a smile.

"Funny, Mom."

She thought maybe one of his school friends had given him some candy or something.

Gabriel disappeared, and Maggie enjoyed some adult talk with Miss Vonda while she ate her ham and mustard sandwich.

A couple of minutes later, he returned. "You done yet?" he asked.

"I'll be there in a minute." She rolled her eyes to Miss Vonda.

"I'm waiting for you." Gabriel ran back down the hallway.

"His present is quite amazing, dear," Miss Vonda said as she put the condiments back in the refrigerator.

"Well, then I definitely want to see this." Her curiosity piqued, she walked through the house and into their small bedroom they shared. She pushed the door open and found Gabriel staring at the wall over his cot.

"Okay, Gabe. I'm all yours. What did you get for your birthday?"

He pointed to a painting hanging on the wall—a painting she had never seen before. Her jaw flew open.

"*This* is your birthday gift? Who . . . where . . . where did this come from? It's amazing." Maggie leaned in for a closer look, fixated with awe on the magnificent art.

"Miss Collingsworth gave it to me today. She painted it for *me*."

"Your teacher?"

"Yeah!"

"Can I take it down so I can see it better in the light?"

"I'll get it, Mom." Gabriel stood on his cot and carefully lowered the painting off of the wall hook.

"You have to sit down if you want to look at it," he said.

Maggie sat down on the bed, and Gabriel placed it on her lap.

"Look at the moving water and the detail in the trees. The River almost looks like it's moving," Gabriel said.

She studied the painting further. "Look! Look at the deer! Everything's so life-like . . . and this frame . . ." She kept running her hands over the edges.

"I know, Mom. I told you. It's amazing."

Maggie held each side of the painting and lifted it up for a straight-on look. "The more you look at The River, the more you see," she said, her voice trailing off.

"What does this say? Ack . . . ." She tried to sound out the signature as she looked closer.

"That's her Indian name mom—Aykwa-Aykwanee. It means Great River. Miss Collingsworth knows The River. She grew up at The River. She used to live there . . . like me. When can we go back to The River . . . you know . . . where we lived with Dad?"

"You don't need to worry about that. Our life is in Cairo now, sweetheart."

Maggie turned her attention back to the painting. "This is such a beautiful gift," she said as distant thoughts of Colorado revisited her. In her mind, it was not an option to go back. There were too many painful memories better left imprisoned in Corley Falls.

It was later that afternoon when Gabriel noticed the card tucked behind the painting. He opened the envelope and discovered a note from Miss Collingsworth.

February 24, 1963
To my friend and student Gabriel Clarke,
Happy Birthday! Always remember, you are a special one-of-a-kind work of art. There will never be another you. You are

treasured and loved. Now a piece of me will always be with you.
You are not alone. You are never alone. Great River loves you.

  Aykwa-Aykwanee—Lily Collingsworth

Gabriel didn't say anything about the note, but he knew that he didn't want anyone else to read it. That was between him and the most special person in the world—after his mom, of course.

With Miss Collingsworth's note tucked safely under his pillow, he went to bed that night thankful for the gift he received. He didn't think his birthday could get any better . . . but it did.

CHAPTER 8

A Birthday Gift

Gabriel woke up to the smell of his favorite breakfast cooking—bacon and chocolate chip pancakes. The chocolate chips were a rare treat, but after all, it was his birthday. He was stumbling out of the bedroom when he overheard his mother saying, "Don't you think it's too cold to go?"

"Nah. That sun is going to take us up to the sixties today," replied Mister Earl.

Still wiping the sleep from his eyes, Gabriel stepped into the kitchen.

"There he is! Twelve years old. Happy Birthday, Gabriel!" His mother wiped her hands on a dish towel and gave him a hug. Mister Earl tapped his shoulder with a warm pat.

"You sit here," his mother directed. She pulled out his chair and placed a feast in front of him: a stack of his favorite chocolate chip pancakes, four pieces of bacon, and a tall glass of milk. Then she struck a match and lit a birthday candle in the middle of his pancakes.

She and Mister Earl warbled an off-key rendition of "Happy Birthday, dear Gabriel," causing the birthday boy to turn red with embarrassment, but the smile he wore spoke of his happiness.

"I've got a surprise for you, Gabriel," Mister Earl said, which caught Gabriel off guard.

"Really?" Gabriel didn't think his birthday weekend could get any better, considering the painting he received from Miss Collingsworth the day before.

"Yep. When you're done eating, come see me in the barn."

"Are we going somewhere? I heard Mom say it might be too cold." Gabriel tried to figure out what lay in store for him.

After enjoying every bite of his breakfast, he went out to visit Mister Earl in the barn. Inside the cowshed, shafts of light beamed through the cracks in the wood, illuminating the particles of hay in the air.

"Come on back here," Mister Earl called from behind the tractor. Gabriel followed his voice to find the older man holding a fishing pole in his hand.

"This is for you." He handed the new rod and reel to Gabriel.

Gabriel was in awe as he took a closer look at the shiny rod.

"This is mine?"

"Yep. All yours. That there is a brand new Zebco spin cast reel. It's real easy to cast."

"Thank you so much, Mister Earl. This is so cool!" Gabriel lunged forward and wrapped his arms around him.

"Okay, that's good, that's good." Mister Earl patted him firmly on the back a couple of times.

"What do you say we go try it out today? I have to sell those two pigs out there, and then we can head to The River to give 'er a whirl."

"Alright!" Gabriel jumped up and shouted, and then he took off to show his mother his new gift.

"Mom! Mom!" Gabriel kept shouting as he ran up to the house.

Maggie opened the screen door. "What did you get?"

Gabriel held up the flashy pole.

"Oh, wow! A new fishing pole!"

"Mister Earl said he'd take me to The River to go fishing today. Can I go?"

"Well . . . seeing that it's your birthday . . ." Maggie smiled. "Are you guys going to go catch us some dinner?"

"Of course, we are!"

Mister Earl shut the barn door and called out, "Get your clothes changed, Master Gabriel, and help me get these pigs loaded."

"Yes, sir!" he saluted.

It was going to be the best birthday ever.

Spring was in the air a little early this year. They might

have a few more cold days, but it was the type of warm day that portended a welcome change from winter cold to summer warmth. A blue sky mottled with fluffy clouds hung over the landscape. The temperature might reach the high sixties by mid-day, maybe even touch seventy. The promise of spring lifted Gabriel's spirits.

He and Mister Earl loaded two pigs into the back of the pickup and headed down to the pig sale on the border of Oklahoma and Kansas. The transaction was completed quickly, allowing them to reach their real destination in the late morning: The River.

They traveled down the same network of gravel roads, through the woods, to find a spot where they could fish.

"Let's see." Mister Earl scratched his face. "I think we'll try somewhere a little different today." He pulled a sharp left and headed down another trail. New budding branches brushed the top of the truck as they moved through the woods. They exited onto a large expanse where the Arkansas River was in plain sight, just a few hundreds yards away. The tires rolled along the dirty road, crunching baby wildflowers sprouts as they turned. They were about a football field's length from The River when Mister Earl rolled to a stop.

"We'll walk the rest of the way. I'm not sure if it's going to be muddy up ahead."

He shut the engine off.

"Hear that?" he asked Gabriel. "It's my favorite sound—nothing. Nothing but The River moving. You have to listen close to hear it, especially from here. Most folks don't take time to get quiet long enough to listen."

Mister Earl opened his door and took a deep breath. "Ahhh," he said, stretching his arms. "You smell that, young man? It's fish!"

Gabriel giggled as he pulled his knit cap on and climbed out of the truck. They untied their fishing poles, grabbed their buckets and bait, and headed toward The River. Mister Earl said it got easier to catch fish in warmer weather, but that didn't guarantee them success. The older man led Gabriel toward a bend in The River.

"You go ahead and get set here, and I'll go upstream a bit."

Gabriel smiled. "Hey, that's not fair. That means you'll get to the fish first."

"Aw, quit your belly achin'," he said with a matching grin.

They got set in their places and began to cast their lines into the moving water. All Gabriel could hear was the whirl of the fishing line with each cast. There was nothing around for miles.

Ten minutes later, Gabriel heard something in the distance—a low-pitched growl. They both heard it at the same time and turned to see what the noise was.

Gabriel turned toward the truck and spotted a large dog— or was it a wolf? His heart began to pound. The animal—a dog with a long, gray-colored coat with streaks of brown and black—had tucked its head down and was baring its razor white teeth, growling aggressively. The creature's crystal blue eyes glared right at Gabriel. He pawed at the ground and hunched over, ready to launch like a racehorse in the gate.

"Don't move, Gabriel. Just stay still," Mister Earl said with a hushed sense of urgency in his voice.

"He's looking at me, Mister Earl. He's looking at me." Gabriel felt panic rising in his throat.

"He'll leave you alone. Just don't move."

The seconds seemed like minutes as the large dog had them pinned against The River. There was no way out. He began to bark and get even more aggressive as the white foam of his saliva dripped from its jowls.

"Mister Earl! Mister Earl!" Gabriel started to cry.

"Gabriel, no!"

The boy dropped his fishing pole and darted toward a tree about thirty yards away. He didn't get two steps when the dog began to charge. Mister Earl dropped his pole and lumbered as quickly as he could after Gabriel.

Terror struck Gabriel's heart as he realized that he couldn't outrun the dog. He froze in place and cried out in fear. The ferocious animal was within ten yards of Gabriel when he stopped in his tracks and dove to the ground, shaking his head violently. Mister Earl picked up a large stick and ran toward the dog, ready to swing.

"Holy Moly! It's okay, Gabriel. It's okay." Mister Earl held up the stick while keeping a healthy distance from the dog, who was obviously distracted.

"It's a rattler. That dog just saved your life."

The dog dropped the deadly viper and began to circle it as he licked his bloodied chops.

"I've never seen anything quite like that," Mister Earl said.

Gabriel slowly regained his composure.

"Is it dead?"

"Oh yeah, it's in two pieces!"

The body of the snake stopped writhing. Mister Earl took a handkerchief out of his back pocket and reached down and picked up the headless body. Then he held up the carcass like a trophy.

"See? That dog took care of him."

The dog sat down on all fours and started wagging its tail.

"You gave us a good scare, boy," Gabriel said, although he wasn't about to pet the creature.

The dog licked his mouth and stood up. He slowly approached Gabriel in a supplicant manner, tail wagging in happiness. Gabriel remained still and allowed the dog to nuzzle his leg, his tail still wagging. Gabriel, who had been nervous, realized the dog wouldn't hurt him. He stretched out his hand, which the dog licked.

"I guess he likes you!" Mister Earl smiled.

The dog started to scamper around Gabriel, bucking playfully.

"You're not so mean after all," Gabriel said as he cautiously stroked the dog's thick fur. "And you saved my life."

<hr />

After the snake incident, the two fishermen got back to fishing. The dog stayed glued to Gabriel's side. Whenever the boy took a break to the truck, the dog followed. Whenever

Gabriel waded into the stream, the dog stood alert on the riverbank. More than once, Mister Earl tried to shoo him away and send him home, but the dog wouldn't leave.

"This dog has no collar. He probably doesn't have a home," Gabriel commented as they packed up their fishing gear.

"He's probably a stray. By the looks of how he handled that snake, I'd say he's pretty wild."

"Mister Earl . . ."

"Don't even think about it, young man."

"Come on! You can see he likes me! He won't be any trouble. I'll take care of him."

"That dog has mischief written all over him. I don't want him after my chickens. Or worse yet, turning on you or the ladies."

"We can make him a pen out back. I'll feed him and . . . and if he steals a chicken, I'll pay for it."

"With what?"

"I'll do extra chores . . . please?" Gabriel was relentless.

"Your momma will kill me."

"I've never had my own animal before. Besides, he saved my life! We can't just leave him out here by himself."

Mister Earl walked back up to The River to rinse out one of the buckets. Gabriel sat patiently on the tailgate. When Mister Earl came back, the dog was lying next to the boy with his head resting on his lap, panting contentedly.

"Listen. If your momma says 'no,' then he's gotta go to the pound."

"Yes, sir!"

Gabriel turned toward the dog. "Did you hear that? You're going home with me!"

They finished putting the gear back in the truck as well as the large canine. Time to head home.

"Just to be sure, when we get to the first town, we're gonna need to post a couple of signs describing the dog we found in case there's an owner who wants to claim him."

"Okay. But he didn't have a collar or anything."

"It doesn't matter. It's the right thing to do. He ain't yours until nobody claims him."

After about thirty minutes of driving, they arrived in Kiowa, Kansas. Mister Earl wrote down a brief description of the dog and the farm's telephone number and posted it at the local diner.

After another several minutes of silent driving, Mister Earl spoke up.

"What are you going to name him?"

Gabriel thought for a moment.

"What about Rio Sky?"

"That was fast. Where'd you come up with that?"

"Well, we found him at The River. Miss Collingsworth told me Rio is another word for river, and his eyes look like they have the sky in them. So Rio Sky will be his full name, but I'll call him Rio for short."

"I like it. Rio Sky it is."

After leaving another notice at an AFW Veteran's hall, Mister Earl said, "I guess you've had quite a birthday."

"Best I ever had."

------◆------

With a new fishing pole and his own dog, Gabriel couldn't get enough of The River that spring and summer. He loved going there. New surprises were waiting for him with every visit. Everything was magical—the way The River sounded, the way it smelled, and the way it "spoke" as Mister Earl said it would. The River was constant and unceasing, yet it had a fresh creativity with each encounter. He now knew why Mister Earl used to say that a visit to The River was always worth the effort.

As for the dog, Maggie was skeptical at first, but Rio Sky became part of their small family after no one responded to Mister Earl's signs. Once she saw how much Gabriel loved his dog, she knew he was an extraordinary gift. Rio gave Gabriel friendship and strength. Everyone could tell his confidence had grown, especially the boys at The Pond. When they saw him with Rio, their respect level skyrocketed.

The best thing of all was that Rio Sky never turned Gabriel away. He always had time, and he always listened to everything Gabriel wanted to talk about—which was a lot.

CHAPTER 9

⟲ The Phone Call ⟳

Time didn't move too quickly during Gabriel's middle and high school years. Even though his teachers told him, "These are the best years of your life," Gabriel felt like he was pedaling on a stationary bike—expending energy but not really going anywhere. Then life ground to a halt after he graduated from Cairo High.

From his vantage point, everyone but him moved on to better things. Many from the Class of '69 headed off to college or the big city to try their luck. Others apprenticed at the family business or worked the family farm, but Gabriel was stuck in downtown Cairo, working at the Five & Dime, stocking shelves and cleaning bathrooms.

His mother didn't save any money for his higher education because she couldn't, even after picking up a second job answering phones for an insurance agency in town. She worked several afternoons a week after the lunch crowd cleared out of the restaurant.

Mister Earl was aging into his eighties, and the fishing trips to The River were fewer and farther between. Miss Vonda was slowing down, period. Everyone was slowing down, and Gabriel languished as well.

For him, the sense of loneliness and isolation was unbearable at times, but he didn't know how to unlock the chains. The scars and rejection he felt from a tumultuous adolescence compounded his lingering grief and relentless fear.

When he could—if no one was around—Gabriel retreated into his thoughts. They were the only safe place in his life, the only place he could control. Indifferent to the world and his future, Gabriel plodded along, performing the same routines day in and day out: chores at the farm, cleaning up at the variety store, and little else. At twenty years of age, he was a shell of the person who came alive when he met the Magic River Man or when he caught his first catfish with Mister Earl.

"Gabriel, does the supply room look clean to you?"

Fred Baggers, the store owner, interrupted Gabriel's daydream.

"Uh, no sir," he replied. That was always the safe answer.

"I'm going to the post office and will be back in half an hour. I want everything spic and span by the time I get back." Mr. Baggers, who had purchased the Five & Dime seventeen years ago, was a prickly, overweight bald man with an uneven mustache. Mister B, as Gabriel called him, always had a way of making most folks feel like they were two feet tall.

Gabriel was heading over to the supply room to check things out when the store phone rang.

"Five and Dime," Gabriel stated curtly.

"Is Gabriel Clarke there?" a confident male voice asked.

"Yeah. I'm Gabriel."

"Hey, big guy. What are you doing?"

"Who is this?"

"Ah, come on. You don't know? I'll give you five bucks if you can guess."

Gabriel was intrigued. No one ever called him at the store—or at the farm. Then something about the brusque voice tripped his memory.

"Jimmy?"

"Bingo!"

Gabriel smiled in disbelief. Jimmy Bly, his childhood friend, was on the line. They hadn't talked much since Jimmy went off to college a couple of years ago.

The conversation quickly became one-sided as Jimmy regaled Gabriel on what campus life was like at the University of Kansas—the Jayhawks football games, the late nights, and the cute girls in the sororities. Then Gabriel remembered: Jimmy was a pied piper of sorts. Ever since he had known him in grade school, his friend had a certain way with people and often went out of his way to include Gabriel in his circle of influence. Gabriel was never sure why, but he was grateful.

"Some guys in my fraternity are organizing a big trip out west before the spring semester is over, and I want you to join us."

"A trip doing what?" Gabriel wasn't very interested in going, but he had to at least pretend that it sounded like fun.

"We're heading to Colorado for hiking and camping. Maybe a little rafting, too, if the weather cooperates. You gotta come, man! We'll have a blast. Just chip in a few bucks for gas and food, and you'll be covered. I'm swinging by Cairo to see my parents, so I can give you a ride. We're leaving two weeks from today. You in?"

Gabriel was filled with mixed emotions. The thought of going on an out-of-town trip and meeting new people created butterflies in his stomach. He couldn't see how *he* could go camping in the Colorado Rockies. All he had known from the time he was four years old was the farm in Kansas and those occasional day trips to the Kansas-Oklahoma border to fish in the Arkansas River with Mister Earl.

"Uh, I don't know Jimmy. I've got a lot going on. My mom needs me at the farm 'cuz Mister Earl is getting older. And I don't think Mister B would give me the time off."

"Aw, come on, man! Seriously, you need a break. You haven't left that farm since I've known ya. Besides, one of my buddies said he has a friend out there who is guaranteeing to introduce us to a few of the local girls. What do you say? I'm not taking no for an answer, by the way."

Gabriel chuckled nervously. Jimmy could be awfully persuasive.

"Okay, okay. Let me do some checking at the store and get back to you. I hope I don't regret this, though. Colorado is a long way."

"You'll never know what it's like out there if you stay in Cairo, buddy. You gotta take some chances sometimes. It's called *living*. Call me at the Sigma Chi house. I'll see ya."

Gabriel made his way to the supply closet. His mind was racing at the possibilities of disaster . . . and fun. He opened the door to the supply room and flicked on the light. He glanced around the dingy concrete room at all the lifeless clutter—the mops and brooms, the cleaning supplies, the boxes of retail stock, and a few dead bugs upside down in the corner. He began to feel the discontent of his existence closing in on him. It would be great to get a break from the broom and Mister B.

Even if Mister B doesn't give me the time off. He can fire me if he wants. Mom and Mister Earl will just have to manage the farm without me. It's just for a few days anyway.

I've got to get out of Kansas.

It's time.

<hr />

It was daybreak, a lazy late May morning in Cairo. Already, the air was thick and warm, a harbinger of summer-like heat to come. To the east, an orange glow was fading into the azure blue ceiling over the farm.

Gabriel woke at the crack of dawn, a little nervous but excited, too. He wasn't worried about Jimmy, even though his old friend was probably as full of craziness and mischief in college as he was in high school. Jimmy liked to take things to the limit—just to find where the boundaries lay. He liked life to be a little dangerous, and that feeling was infectious for those in his orbit.

Gabriel wouldn't even have even considered this trip if it weren't for Jimmy. Once again, even though he hadn't really seen Jimmy since high school graduation, his old buddy was including him in one of his activities. He didn't have to do that, but he did.

Jimmy used to say, "Life is meant to be lived together. 'Together' is where the best stuff happens." Perhaps his old friend knew he was shy, dating back to the time in elementary school when Gabriel wanted to stay on the sidelines for the big wrestling matches at The Pond. Either way, Jimmy *lived* his words.

After not seeing Jimmy for several years, getting that phone call was like an infusion of light in a pitch-black room. For all of Gabriel's twenty years, he felt like an outsider, left alone to fend for himself. He was grateful for his mom and the Cartwrights, but something profound was missing. He felt like he was looking at life through the bottom of a Coke bottle— blurry and ill-formed. It was like he could see laughter and joy on the other side of the thick glass, but he couldn't hear or experience it.

Maybe this trip to Colorado would shatter that glass forever.

He could only hope.

At about 6:45 a.m., the peaceful silence of the cornfields was broken by the jarring sound of a 1964 two-tone red-and-white Chevrolet Corvair 95 van swerving into the farm like a getaway car running from the law. Jimmy Bly was behind the wheel.

He wasn't alone.

Inside the van were three other guys with shaggy hair and scruffy faces, and all manner of camping gear was tied to the roof. The Corvair kicked up clouds of dust as the van slid to a stop about thirty yards in front of the farmhouse. Jimmy leaned half of his body out of the van window to summon Gabriel.

"Gabriel! Let's go, my brother! Adventure awaits!"

Gabriel was taking the last couple of bites of the eggs and bacon that his mother had fixed him when Mister Earl knocked and walked into their kitchen.

"Those boys sure are loud for this early in the mornin'," he grumbled.

Gabriel was heading out the front door toward the van when Jimmy jumped out of the truck, opened his arms, and yelled, "What's up brother?"

The spontaneous greeting made Gabriel feel like a million bucks. He smiled and received one of Jimmy's famous bear hugs.

"Let me go get my stuff," he said, and Gabriel ran back into the house to retrieve his duffel bag. Rio stood up on the front porch and wagged his tail, excited by all the activity.

"Bye, Mom!" he said, as he gave her a quick hug. "We'll be back in no time."

Gabriel climbed into the side door of the van. Then Miss Vonda appeared on the porch, holding a picnic basket.

"Wait—I got some homemade sweet rolls and snacks." She waddled down the front porch steps toward the van.

Gabriel jumped out to fetch the wicker basket. "Thanks, Miss Vonda."

"We have an extra seat in the van if you'd like to join us," Jimmy yelled out. "We could use some cooking help around the campfire!"

Miss Vonda batted her hand in the air and gave Jimmy a coy grin.

The guys sitting next to the windows leaned out and started slapping the side of the van as they pulled out. Gabriel peered out the back window to see his mother and the Cartwrights standing on the porch, getting smaller and smaller. The guys hooted and hollered like rebel rousers off to a party.

Am I really doing this? Going all the way to Colorado with a bunch of guys I don't even know?

Gabriel had a smile on the outside, but inside, his guts were churning.

He felt better after Jimmy's friends introduced themselves to him during the first hour of driving. Each one was quite gregarious and confident:

• Brian James, aka "Cig," sat in the front seat. He never took an unlit cigarette out of his mouth, hence his nickname. He could chew gum, drink soda, and talk about the origins of the universe without dropping the cigarette from his lips. Portly, with black bushy hair and a beard that seemed to cover his entire face except for his eyes, Cig was a quirky intellectual who didn't say much but was quite funny when he did.

• Redhead Stevie Jones took up the van's rear bench seat. He had slightly bucked teeth, lots of freckles, long red sideburns, and a lanky build. He might have weighed 130 pounds soaking wet. Stevie always seemed to take the brunt of the jokes, but he didn't mind. When he wasn't in school, he worked at his father's shoe store in Topeka. Jimmy said he was smart at the business stuff.

A childhood nickname had followed him all the way to college—Stink. He got the nickname when he was ten years old and lost a bet. It seems that one time he had to chase a skunk out of its home in a hollowed-out log. Stevie got sprayed . . . and he stunk for *days*.

• Last but not least was Rollie Sever, who didn't lack for self-confidence with the ladies. He was about six feet tall with perfectly feathered wavy brown locks, dark brown eyes with plenty of soul, and a too-cool-for-school attitude. His ego was bigger than his hair.

His air of self-assurance drew girls to him like a magnet. Jimmy would always tease him about his constant neglect of buttoning the top three buttons of his shirt. He was quite proud of his chest and the grizzly-like hair growing on it.

So Jimmy Bly, Brian "Cig" James, Stevie "Stink" Jones, Rollie Sever, and Gabriel Clarke set out on their road trip to Colorado. With sweet rolls, a cooler of soda, and a welcome opportunity to have some fun and make some memories, Gabriel hoped this trip to The River would change everything for him.

CHAPTER 10

The Trip to the River

Gabriel had never seen an orange sun fall beneath the jagged-tooth skyline of a mountain range before, but he was exhilarated by the sight.

They had pulled off the main highway thirty minutes earlier onto a winding gravel road that would lead them to their campsite. During the overnight part of their trip, he and the guys had traded off napping for a couple hours while they took turns staying up with the driver. Jimmy drove most of the time, but even the great Bly needed a break from time to time.

"Almost there, fellas!" Jimmy blurted with excitement.

Everybody came to their senses and was excited to finally arrive and get out of the van after nearly two days of driving. Their campsite was in an area of Splash Canyon known as "The Beach" to locals. The dirt road got narrower as the van moseyed deeper into the forest. Up one steep grade and down another, the further they traveled, the stranger Gabriel felt, however.

"How much longer?" he asked nervously.

"Only five or ten minutes," replied Jimmy. "Wait till you see this place. It's amazing." His soothing words calmed Gabriel.

Turns out Jimmy was right. As they pulled through the last clump of tall fir and large spruce trees, the forest opened to an incredible scene that took Gabriel's breath away. It was like Mother Nature had raised the curtain to reveal a theatrical stage like no other. They parked the van and immediately started looking around like little kids at an amusement park for the first time.

"Amazing," said Brian "Cig" James.

"It's like a postcard!" exclaimed Rollie Sever.

All of the guys were going on and on about the natural panorama surrounding them, but Gabriel remained quiet because he was soaking in the beauty of the canyon. The Beach was just that—an opening along The River where the forest dissolved into a sandy clay floor, one hundred feet wide and about a quarter of a mile long. Since the riverbed gradient was slight, the water flowed steady and calm, bubbling over the rocks and creating a sonic backdrop to soothe the soul.

Beautiful hues of light reflected through the trees, and being inside the gorge was like being in another world. Gabriel walked up to The River's edge and saw the stream and the canyon curl to his left, which was five hundred yards downstream. He could hear in the distance a dull roar from the thundering falls that were around the corner.

The Beach was nestled in the crook of the bottom of a

horseshoe that The River had carved through the canyon. On the other side of the water, the canyon walls rose sharply into the sky—way over five hundred feet. Boulders both sharp and round covered the canyon walls like a reddish brown tapestry, with trees jutting out and shooting toward the heavens like skyscrapers in the big city. All he could hear was the occasional screech of an eagle and the soothing sound of rippling water flowing by. There were no city or traffic noises. To Gabriel, this was untouched heaven on earth.

When Gabriel inhaled the beauty of The River, he locked eyes with the water and time stood still. He couldn't shift his gaze. Then his heart beat faster and faster as he began to recall episodes from his childhood. Like flash cards of memory, he saw happy images of The River that he had experienced as a young child. He saw his father and grandfather working at their camp, fixing rafts and planning trips. The smell of the forest pine and the crisp air reminded him of everything that was good at The River.

Then in an instant, like images from a horror movie trailer, flashes of light and scenes from the day The River took his dad crowded out the beauty he was experiencing. The breadth of emotion he was feeling was all-consuming. His heart began to race even more, and he couldn't catch his breath. It was like the canyon walls were closing in on him, but he didn't want to let the other guys know what he was going through. He turned his back to The River and started walking toward the van.

"Where you going?" Jimmy asked.

"Just taking a walk," Gabriel replied as he tried to deal with the fear and panic crushing his chest.

More thoughts ran through Gabriel's mind as he coped with his anxiety.

I can't do this.

Why do I feel this way?

I want to go back to Kansas.

He could hear the muffled conversations the guys were having by the water as they skipped rocks off the surface of the placid water and washed their faces in the crystal-clear flow. He wanted to be part of them. Gabriel managed to regain his composure as the bad thoughts faded into the background. He helped himself to a Nesbitt from the cooler and returned to The River's edge, where he sat down on a fallen tree stump and tried once again to enjoy the beauty of the wilderness.

Jimmy clapped his hands. "Let's unload and set up camp so we can party, boys! We have only about an hour before it's dark."

Jimmy was the initiator for almost everything. In quick order, the guys untied the tarp that covered the gear strapped to the roof of the van. In no time at all, they unloaded three tents, five sleeping bags, five beach chairs, two coolers, several lanterns, and assorted camping paraphernalia.

"Stink, you were an Eagle Scout, right?" Jimmy was directing traffic again. "Why don't you and Gabriel get the fire started, and the rest of us will work on the tents."

"Right on, man!" Stink said. "I love making fire. It's a legitimate art form!"

Everybody always responded well to Jimmy's delegation

efforts, although Rollie needed to hear things two or three times before he kicked into gear. Gabriel noticed that every chance he got, he checked out his hairdo in the side mirror of the van.

For his part, Gabriel gathered wood while Stink searched for rocks that could be used to ring a fire pit. Within fifteen minutes, they had a fire going, just about the same time that two more vanloads arrived. They were all friends or acquaintances of Jimmy's. Gabriel watched them step out of the rear seat of the vans like soldiers coming out of a 'Nam transport helicopter. They were guys, but Gabriel was pleased that some girls had come along, too.

It was the last girl getting out of the second van who caught his eye. Her long, wavy auburn hair flowed out of a faded orange bandana, and she had a rock climber's lean body and tan skin. She wore army green hiking shorts and a long-sleeve tie-dye shirt with a jeans jacket tied around her waist.

Gabriel, carrying an armload of twigs and dead branches, was mesmerized by what he saw. His mouth parted as he watched her come in his direction. She had high cheekbones framed by light green eyes and thick eyebrows but wore no make-up. She didn't need any. He was so spellbound that it was like she was moving in slow motion.

Gabriel stepped in her direction, and their eyes locked for a brief moment. She smiled and raised her eyebrows as if to say, *Hello, it's nice to see you, but your staring at me is a little weird.*

Nothing ever got by Cig, who picked up on what was

happening from The Beach. "Hey, wipe your chin, Gabriel!"

Some of the guys laughed, and Gabriel wanted to crawl into a hole. How embarrassing! He quickly looked away and dropped the twigs onto the pile next to the fire pit. *She must think I'm an idiot. I can't believe it. I just stared at her.*

For the rest of the evening, he faded into the background as his thoughts and insecurity got the best of him. If nobody noticed him the rest of the trip, that would be fine with him.

———◆———

It was about 10:30 p.m., and all the tents were set up. The night sky was clear, and the stars were magnificent. The moon was vivid and so massive that the bright white orb looked like it was almost too close to Earth. The fire was roaring at least five feet high, and everyone had gathered around the warm flames, talking and sipping on various libations—beer being the most popular.

At this altitude, there was a nip in the air. When the sun went down behind the canyon walls, the temperature would drop a good twenty-five or thirty degrees. Rollie, of course, had two girls next to him to keep him warm, and they were chatting and giggling like eight-year-olds. Cig broke out his baritone ukulele and launched into his repertoire of folk tunes.

Gabriel just took it all in and enjoyed the distraction of watching the others interacting. He hadn't summoned the courage to say anything to the cute girl who had caught his attention earlier. He noticed that she seemed so comfortable with everyone. Just by watching her, Gabriel could tell she was kind, self-confident, and unfazed by her surroundings or the people on the trip. She looked everyone in the eye when she spoke, and her laugh was contagious. Throughout the evening, all of the guys made an effort to interact with her, making stupid jokes or the typical icebreaker comments, but she handled the situations with aplomb.

I hope I get to talk to her, he thought. *I don't know what I'd say, though. Probably something stupid. She doesn't even know I'm here.*

Gabriel turned his attention to a conversation he overheard with Jimmy and a couple of the new guys.

"Tomorrow we'll go to The Cliffs and have some fun. You guys are going to scream like little girls," Jimmy said.

Gabriel decided this was a conversation he wanted to join. "What cliffs?" he asked.

"It's this amazing place about a two-mile hike from here. There are forty- and fifty-foot cliffs jutting out over The River. The water is deep and swirling. You just jump off and swim. Long way down, but it's awesome."

Gabriel began thinking of a way out. He could swim, but he wasn't fond of the water that much—or jumping from heights. He had actually been afraid of water when he was a kid, so he began to think of ways he could stay behind.

Midnight was approaching. The fire was dying down, and the long day of travel was catching up with everyone. They made their way back to their tents spread out on The Beach and the edge of the forest. Gabriel was sharing a large tent with Jimmy. They got into their sleeping bags and extinguished the lantern.

"Man, I think I'm wasted," Jimmy slurred.

Gabriel chuckled. Jimmy was known for enjoying one—make that a few—too many. Thirty seconds later, Jimmy was out. The camp got eerily quiet in a matter of minutes. All Gabriel could hear against the soundtrack of The River was the crackle of the fire as the embers consumed the small logs and twigs.

Gabriel was quite tired, but he lay there for nearly an hour unable to sleep. Camping wasn't something he had done much of, so sleeping on the ground, out in the wilderness with only a thin nylon tent separating him from the wild, did not feel comfortable at all.

There has to be all sorts of savage animals out there.

As he lay in the tent, alone with his thoughts, he heard what sounded like a splash in the water. *That didn't sound right.* Then he heard another splash—and another.

Could that be a bear playing in the water?

His curiosity propelled him to go investigate. He slid out of his sleeping bag, unzipped the tent, and peered toward The River. The ambient light from the fire and the glow of the brilliant moon lit the canyon. But he saw nothing. The water was flowing smoothly, just as it was when he turned in more than an hour ago.

Gabriel looked around the camp. Everyone was still asleep. He got an eerie feeling that he was not alone. At first, he was a bit frightened, but he felt drawn to walk around and check things out. His eyes scanned the campground and The River, but nothing looked amiss. He approached the fire to warm himself when it happened again. The waters at the center of The River began to swirl slowly in a large circle—about the size of the van they had driven from Kansas. It was as if some huge cosmic spoon was stirring the water.

There's no fish that big in The River. Maybe it's a weird current. Or am I dreaming all this?

Gabriel's heart pounded as the sound of the swirling water increased in speed and intensity. The motion of the water created a deepening hole in the center of the swirl. He couldn't stop watching as the swirling got stronger and stronger, louder and louder, and then . . . it just stopped.

Gabriel looked around to see if any of the commotion had disturbed anyone else. Not a peep came from the tents. He couldn't believe what he had just seen. While it was terrifying, he somehow felt comforted by what he witnessed. It was like he was allowed to experience something unique to him.

He sat down by the fire and decided to lay down on his jacket and look at the stars. He felt warm, even though he was dressed in boxers and a T-shirt. In fact, the temperature felt as warm as the middle of the afternoon even though it was the middle of the night.

"Gabriel . . . Gabriel! What are you doing out here?"

Jimmy shook Gabriel's shoulder. The sun was up, and sunlight filtered through the fir trees. Gabriel opened his eyes with a bewildered look on his face.

"I must have fallen asleep."

"Man, you're nuts! You've gotta be freezing!"

Gabriel looked around. A few people were starting to stir from their tents, but no one was paying attention to them.

"No, I feel fine. I guess I got hot in my sleeping bag."

"You're crazy. It was too cold to sleep outside last night without a sleeping bag."

"Well, I did."

Gabriel wasn't about to tell Jimmy what had happened to him the night before. He couldn't explain it anyway because he wasn't even sure what had happened.

Was it all a dream? Was I sleepwalking?

For some reason, though, he felt comforted by what he experienced during the night. He wasn't scared at all.

He had made a connection with The River.

CHAPTER 11

THE GIRL

The sun was still hidden behind the canyon walls, but its light spilled onto The Beach, warming the campers who were starting to rise and shine. The campfire was down to smoldering coals, so Gabriel gathered dead twigs and branches to revive their fire so they could cook breakfast.

One thing he learned from Mister Earl was good fire-making techniques. Back on the farm, the older man would always say, "Workin' a good fire will keep a man's mind in a good place."

Gabriel never forgot that. After he got the fire going again, he walked to the edge of The River and looked out into the middle of the wide stream, at the place where he saw the stirring the night before. He began to daydream about what he experienced. He still wasn't completely positive that the event really happened, but what he saw with his eyes seemed so real: the stirring, the warmth, the wind, and the feeling that someone was with him.

"Hey, bro," a hushed voice said out of nowhere.

Gabriel's heart skipped a beat. He was so focused on The River that he didn't hear Cig walk up behind him.

"You trying to kill me, man? You scared me to death."

Cig grinned. "You know where that iron skillet is to fry the bacon? I can't have eggs without bacon."

"I think it's in Jimmy's box in the back of the van." Gabriel knew he spoke with a tinge of agitation as he pointed toward the parked vehicle.

"You need some more sleep, Sunshine?" Cig turned the corner of his mouth down. "Cheer up. You'll thank me once you taste the food."

As Gabriel turned away, something caught his eye over The River. The light from the sun was getting so bright that he cupped his right hand and touched his forehead to shade his eyes. There, swirling in the sky, was a huge beautiful bird, pure white in color with a few black markings on its chest along with a reddish tail feather.

The bird majestically circled about one hundred feet off of the water in a slow drifting manner that looked completely effortless. Then the raptor slowly spiraled its way closer and closer to the water. The way the bird maintained its steady downward trajectory was magnificent.

Gabriel was engrossed watching the incredible creature glide over The River. His concentration was interrupted by a female voice. "It's a red-tailed hawk—an albino red-tailed hawk, that is. Isn't it beautiful?"

Gabriel turned. It was the same girl he'd stared at the night before. His heart rate doubled—and he couldn't speak. He didn't know what to say.

"Ah . . . amazing," was all he could muster.

"Those birds are very rare. They look so mysterious, don't they? The way they come and go as they please. I love to watch them soar."

The pure white hawk circled The River until it was about five feet above the water in precisely the same place Gabriel saw the stirring the night before. The hawk floated over the current for another minute before powerfully flapping its wings to ascend out of the canyon.

When the majestic creature was gone from their sight, the girl broke the silence.

"I'm Tabitha." She held out her hand to shake Gabriel's.

"Hi." Gabriel shook her hand quickly, but he felt embarrassed.

"And your name is—?" Tabitha raised her distinctive eyebrows.

"Oh, right . . . Gabriel . . . Gabriel Clarke."

"You don't say much do you?"

"I guess not." He threw a rock into the water.

"Man of few words. I like that. So are you going with us to The Cliffs? It's beautiful up there. I hike there all the time since I live in these parts. You should come with us. The Cliffs are quite breathtaking . . . and fun too."

Gabriel wasn't convinced. "Maybe I'll go. Or maybe I'll stay behind and take care of the camp."

"Oh, come on! You have to go. It'll be fun. I guarantee it. Besides, I've got to have someone else to talk to. I can take only so much of those meatheads over there."

Gabriel enjoyed her flirtatious tone. He had never experienced a girl like this.

She is talking to me. She is asking me to do something with her. Gabriel could hardly believe what was happening—a fresh start with someone who didn't know the issues he'd been struggling with throughout his life.

"Where are you from, Gabriel Clarke?" Tabitha kept engaging him in conversation, but he kept staring at The River.

"Cairo, Kansas," he said after a long silence. "I've lived there since I was four years old. Cairo sure doesn't look like this."

Tabitha came alongside him and placed her left hand inside Gabriel's right bicep, just above his elbow. The simple movement sent shivers up and down his body.

"Let's get some coffee. You like coffee?" She started to lead him toward the campfire.

"Sure."

She squeezed his arm. "Wow, you're strong. Do you lift weights or something?"

"Just working on the farm, I guess. My dad was really strong. I probably got it from him."

"I'd say your father was every bit of six feet, broad shouldered, with clear blue eyes and wavy blond hair. Am I right?" Tabitha asked in a playful manner.

Gabriel knew he was blushing. "I mean, if you say so—"

"And your dad must have tanned well."

Gabriel relaxed and smiled. He felt like a different person with Tabitha. He actually felt good about himself. She was making him forget about his insecurity and his boring life. Being with her was like being in heaven.

A loud voice pierced the solitude of the wilderness.

"Cig's world-famous camping coffee is ready! Come and get it, earthlings!"

The bearded one cupped his hand over his mouth like a megaphone as he shouted for everyone to get out of their tents and up and at 'em. The camp stirred, and one by one, sleepy-headed individuals approached the campfire with tin mugs in hand. Anyone could see that Cig was proud of his coffee—so thick that one could probably drop a rock in and watch it float. Drinking Cig's motor oil added to the ambience.

Cig and Jimmy got the bacon and eggs going—cooking the bacon first and then breaking eggs into the bacon grease in an iron skillet. People sat on logs and ate their breakfast, and after an appropriate amount of time had passed, Jimmy said he had an announcement to make.

"Listen up, guys. We're going to take off for The Cliffs in about thirty minutes, so please be ready."

Gabriel was still undecided about whether he would go. He was feeling a bit nauseous and wasn't sure why. Meeting and talking with Tabitha complicated matters. He could feel himself slipping into that place in his mind where it was hard to recover.

Here I am, getting out of Kansas for the first time in fifteen years, traveling to the most beautiful place I've ever seen, meeting new friends, and I'm a mess. Why am I feeling down? Why can't I just live!

His mind and emotions were quarreling with each other. It was like he was in a quicksand trap of the soul and was just begging for someone to throw him a rope, but he didn't know how to ask. There were occasions when he would be on the cusp of breaking free and enjoying life, but then he would get sabotaged by his pain. Other times, even in the best of circumstances, a cloak of sadness would fall over him like a two hundred-pound coat that he couldn't shake off. He dragged his pain with him wherever he went.

His sadness would often turn to fear: fear of the unknown, fear that he would never know peace, fear of being alone, and even fear of dying. His fear would then turn to anger, but anger at himself. Anger that he didn't have his dad. Anger for not saving his father that fateful day. Anger at those stupid kayakers for not knowing there were huge falls ahead. And blazing anger at The River for taking Dad so early in his life.

His anger was a vicious storm, and he needed to run for cover in his secret place—just like he did when he was a child.

It was looking like today was another one of those days.

Everyone had gotten their packs on and was ready to depart for their daylong journey to The Cliffs. Gabriel had kept himself busy picking up around the camp, tending to the fire, and occasionally skipping rocks on The River, hoping folks wouldn't notice that he wasn't packing to go.

"Let's do this!" Jimmy yelled out from across the beach.

The pack of college students and local girls began to fall in line and follow Jimmy to the edge of the woods. Tabitha was up in front with everyone else. Before Jimmy entered the woods, he glanced back one final time.

Gabriel was standing next to The River—and no backpack to be seen.

"Gabriel! Hey, man, are you coming?" Jimmy shouted.

Tabitha waved her arm at him, motioning for him to join them.

Gabriel looked in their direction. "I'm not feeling so hot. I'm gonna stay here and keep an eye on things. I'll catch up with you guys when you get back."

"You sure?" There was a bit of concern in Jimmy's voice.

"Yep. See ya when you get back."

"Okay, man. Suit yourself."

Tabitha looked back, and Gabriel saw that her countenance had dropped. As he watched her and the others climb up the first steep grade and disappear into the towering fir and spruce trees, his mind and heart became increasingly heavy.

Why can't I push through this? I'm going to miss so much. Why do I do this to myself?

He walked back over to the fire and poked the embers with a stick. He dropped a couple more large branches onto the flames. It took only a few minutes for their echoing conversation and laughter to fade and for the distant hum of the waterfalls around the bend to loom larger.

Gabriel was alone in the beauty of the canyon and alone with his thoughts. He sat down on a thick log that lay on the edge of The Beach. With the massive canyon wall as a backdrop, he faced The River and watched the water move slowly by.

Gabriel's gaze at The River deepened. He leaned back up and put his hands into the pockets of his old hooded sweatshirt and found something—a blue-and-gray Aggie marble, one he'd kept from his childhood. He'd been looking for this marble for years. The Aggie was very special to him, one of his favorites.

He held the marble up to the light, and his mind instantly flashed back to when he and Dad would play marbles at the whitewater camp after his father returned from his river runs. The brown and red cliffs and towering trees of the canyon wall on the other side of The River blurred . . . and a movie screen of Gabriel's imagination began showing scenes from the first years of his life. He could see his father's wide strong hand— with his thumb tucked in the crook of his index finger—getting ready to shoot that marble.

"I'm going to beat you this time, buddy!"

"No way, Dad! No way!"

The interaction played in his mind's eye so vividly he could almost hear the dialogue reverberate in the canyon.

"How come you keep getting taller, Gabe? You better stop growing, or soon you'll be taller and stronger than me!"

"You can't stop me, Dad. I'm going to be bigger than you soon!"

He remembered Dad scooping him up in his arms and tickling him, then nuzzling him on his neck. He could almost feel the scruff of his soft beard against his face. It felt safe to be in his arms. His dad was so strong.

Lost in an endless string of memories, Gabriel thought about how much he missed his father. How much he wanted to experience that kind of love again. The desire to feel the safety of his father's arms one more time.

"Pay attention, Gabe. I'm going to show you this again."

The scene of his father showing him how to tie various rope knots came into view.

The scene cut to the conversation they'd have every Sunday morning at 6:30 a.m. "Daddy, can you make me pancakes today?" Gabriel loved his dad's special applesauce pancakes.

"Sure, buddy." That scene played forth as well as others on the canyon theater.

Then a darker memory crept into his consciousness.

"Gabriel! Stay here. Don't move. I'll be right back."

Gabriel could still feel his father's hand pressing on his chest from that day. It was the last time he felt his father's touch. That was the day his dad made his way down the hill to help the kayakers. The scenes and memories escalated and started moving faster. Gabriel breathed hard, and his heart beat faster. He experienced the helplessness he felt that day. His mind screamed, "Don't go, Dad. Don't go!"

He knew what happened in this memory, but maybe he could stop him this time. He screamed again, but all he could do was watch the events unfold. After the kayaker went over the falls, everything grew silent. The scene played out in slow motion, and all he could feel was the throb of his heartbeat. He watched his father slide down the graveled hill, careful to navigate the trees and rocks. He saw the kayak turned upside down and pinned underneath the rock. He saw his father use a thick branch to push on the kayak.

Then the images flickered and started to fade. Gabriel strained to focus, calling out to his father but to no avail. Like the static of a weak radio signal, the last image Gabriel saw was his father's hand rising out of the water from underneath the rock, desperately grasping for something to pull him out. As the image flickered in his mind, the silence grew deafening.

Gabriel began to weep. His sobs echoed through the canyon. Then, through his uncontrollable anguish, he screamed, "Why? . . . Why? . . . Come back, Daddy! Please come back! Please!"

Gabriel fell to his knees at The River's edge and covered his face with his hands. For several minutes, he stayed there and grieved. He lamented the loss of what could have been. He grieved the loss of his father.

He finally pulled his hands off of his face. Wiping his nose and tears on his sleeve, his eyes were red and swollen.

"Why am I here, at The River?" he said aloud. His grief was turning into anger.

"*You* did this! *You* did this!" Gabriel shouted with deep intensity and pointed at the gentle, flowing water. "*You* took him away!"

Gabriel picked up anything he could find to throw into the River. He heaved stray branches and handfuls of sand. He picked up a large rock, raised it over his head with both hands, and threw it into the moving water, but his effort carried him to The River's edge.

He stumbled and splashed, then fell into knee-deep water. He stood up and kicked the water with everything he had. He kept on kicking and flailing away until he was completely exhausted. Then he dropped to his knees and gulped huge breaths and sobbed. With flecks of mud splattered on his face and his hair dripping wet, all he could hear was the sound of his breathing and the unfazed flow of The River.

Just then, Gabriel heard a loud screech echo through the canyon. He looked high above and saw the majestic creature again—the red-tailed white hawk, gliding in a giant circle at least five hundred feet up.

A warm wind blew across The River and into Gabriel's face. The wind wrapped around him. In the twinkle of an eye, Gabriel heard that sound again—the sound he heard last night.

The River began to stir. In a large circular motion, the stirring became faster and faster.

Gabriel was not afraid. This time, his heartbeat slowed down, and he felt that he was not alone.

CHAPTER 12

The River Speaks

With arms stretched over his head and lying in the sand like a worn-out ragdoll, Gabriel stared up at the sky, exhausted and emotionally wrenched. He lay just a few feet from The River, contemplating everything he had felt in the last few moments. He sensed a release of years of pent-up emotion, even if only The River and the canyon walls had heard his pleas.

The words of Mister Earl came back to him. "The River has a way, you know."

***

Gabriel felt the air getting warmer in the canyon. Then, without warning, the water rose rapidly but not violently. The swirling water felt warm to him, and before he knew it, he was submerged up to his shoulders.

But he didn't feel wet. He felt warm.

Gabriel looked around the canyon—up and down and from side to side. What he saw took his breath away. As The River rose in the canyon, he was lifted as well, staying in the water shoulder-deep. He tried to leap onto the shore, but he was powerless. All he could do was watch The River rise and cover The Beach, smothering the fire and the tents.

The scene was surreal . . . spellbinding.

He heard the screech of the white red-tailed hawk. Gabriel looked up and saw the raptor circle overhead and swoop close to him—so close that he could feel the warm air move with each swoosh of its wings.

Then he felt an even stranger sensation. A giant hand of water cupped underneath him as The River rose again. The hand spun him around slowly, and he was now floating.

Gabriel surrendered to the experience, but questions were stacking up in his mind.

The River turned him around so that he was facing the canyon wall and the middle of the stream where the stirring had occurred. He was floating in water that had to be twenty feet above where The Beach used to be.

The light in the canyon grew dim except for a glow on the majestic white hawk. The creature swooped down and touched the water's surface with its talons. Then, with a powerful blast of its wings, the hawk soared into the sky.

With each movement of its sprawling wings, Gabriel could hear the air move throughout the canyon. As the hawk darted to the sky, climbing higher and higher, it was followed by a massive scrim of water and mist. The River erupted like a geyser, sending a sheet of water into the atmosphere and rose as far as the eye could see. The light in the canyon grew even more faint as the wall of water began to light up.

Images started to come into view on the spray of water, but Gabriel couldn't quite make them out. He rubbed his eyes, and the first scene came into focus. He saw their farm in Kansas. Mister Earl was riding his tractor through the fields. The image faded to one of Miss Vonda cooking in the kitchen. Then his mom pulled up the gravel road in her pick-up truck, still dressed in her waitress uniform. Gabriel could hear the sound of the motor running, the tires crunching over the gravel road.

A deep voice gently broke into the soundtrack of his experience. "I've always been with you, Gabriel," said the voice.

Could it be . . . was his father speaking?

"Who's there? Dad? Daddy? Is that you?"

The rich baritone sounded like his dad's voice—deep, strong, and comforting. His questions garnered no responses, however, just more images of his life.

"Say something! Is that you?"

Nothing.

"Why did you leave me that day? Why did you jump in the water?" Gabriel's eyes filled with tears again.

"I've missed you!" he cried out in pain. "I've needed you, and you weren't there! Those kayakers deserved whatever happened to them. *Wasn't I more important than them?*"

He heard no reply. The image then morphed into an old

man in bib overalls with a long gray beard, sitting in a rocking chair while he sallied back and forth. A sign over his head said, "Magic River Marbles." Then quickly the scene turned to him fishing on the Arkansas River with Mister Earl. Then on to his elementary school days when he met Miss Collingsworth for the first time. Those were all great memories, but Gabriel wanted his questions answered.

Then the images disappeared, and Gabriel could hear the voice of a small child in the distance.

"Daddy! Daddy!"

The water screen lit up again. This time, there was a picture of a large hiking boot digging into the rocky soil. Rivulets of water ran underneath the boot. Then in slow motion, the hiking boot slipped in the muddy soil. Gabriel saw the boot blur and a body fall into the water. Then the scene shifted and showed his father slipping into the current.

Everything became clear to Gabriel. His dad didn't just jump into The River and abandon him. He never intended to strand his boy on the hill that day. He had slipped and fallen into the turbulent current.

The huge face of a beautiful dog came into view. With its eyes blinking and its tongue hanging out, Gabriel recognized him. It was Rio. The camera lens zoomed out, and he saw Rio standing over a dead snake on the day he met the dog that saved his life. Gabriel watched as the scene changed to several moments during his childhood when Rio comforted him on his hard days.

The scenes on the water screen then disappeared, and a

voice spoke again. Still held by The River, Gabriel closed his eyes and listened, more content and peaceful than he could ever remember.

"You don't have to be afraid anymore," the voice said. "I know you don't understand everything that has happened. You can't. I know you thought you were alone, but you've never been alone. Even when you can't see me, I'm there. Even when you can't hear me, I'm there. You were made for me, Gabriel. You were made for The River. Just like your father was made for me and your grandfather before him. You are mine. Your destiny is with me."

The voice stopped. Gabriel looked intently as one more scene came into view—a scene of him looking over his shoulder on the day he turned ten years old. It was the day he received the beautiful painting of The River from his teacher, Miss Collingsworth, who'd painted it for his birthday. He watched himself turn the painting over, and the image zoomed onto her handwriting. He saw this inscription etched into the misty water screen.

Always remember, you are a special one-of-a-kind work of art. There will never be another you. The River loves you.

Gabriel closed his eyes and experienced the sweetest rest he'd ever known.

"I can't believe you guys did that!"

"That was amazing when Rollie tried to take you off the

cliff with him."

"I thought I'd never reach the water."

The conversations grew louder and louder as the hikers emerged from the forest's edge. Gabriel heard them faintly as he opened his eyes.

"Gabriel!" shouted Jimmy as he appeared through the trees. "You missed an amazing day!"

Jimmy approached as Gabriel rose to his feet. "You been sleeping all day?" he asked.

"Ah, no. I was just taking a little nap."

"It's nearly dinner time. What did you do all day?"

That was a good question. Gabriel's eyes looked around. The camp looked exactly the same as when everyone left earlier that day. The fire was still going. The tents were in their places. Everything was dry, and The River looked normal. But earlier everything had been covered with water. What had exactly happened? Was it a dream? It couldn't have been a dream because it was so real.

The debris and rocks that he threw into The River were right back where they were before he had picked them up. He looked into the sky, but there was no sign of the hawk.

"I don't know, man. I had the craziest dream."

"Well, you look different—like something happened to you."

Gabriel didn't respond, and Jimmy said something about getting ready for dinner.

As the others filed into camp, Cig and Stink came by to say hello, which Gabriel appreciated. While everyone was changing out of wet clothes or getting ready for dinner, Gabriel walked over to The River and peered into the water.

Am I going crazy?

The sun was starting to set behind the canyon wall and caused bits of orange light to color the ripples in the water. About half way across The River and downstream a good ways, he noticed something reflecting the sharp light of the setting sun. The brilliant flickering was coming from a crook in a large moss-covered rock—the size of a four-man pup tent—protruding through The River's surface. He walked down the beach to get a closer look. He couldn't quite make out what the sparkling object was. He jammed his hands into the pockets of his hooded sweatshirt, and without thinking through what he was about to do, Gabriel waded into the water with his clothes and shoes on.

"Hey, man, what are you doing?" Jimmy called out.

"Oh, so now you go swimming," Cig said sarcastically.

Stink issued a warning. "That current is faster than it looks, Gabriel."

Everyone in the campground moved closer to The Beach to watch Gabriel. A rising chorus asked if he was all right.

Gabriel wasn't listening. He was completely focused on that rock. Undeterred, he kept moving. He plodded until he reached waist-high water when the current suddenly lifted him off his footing.

Several girls screamed.

He suddenly realized this might be dangerous since the falls were downstream just around the bend. He tried to regain his footing and stand up, but the water was too strong. A mild panic set in, and he attempted to swim against the current.

That's when he heard a distinctive voice in the distance speaking directly to him.

"Don't fight it, Gabriel. Just let it take you. Go feet first. You'll land on the rock out there."

Tabitha spoke with authority, as if she knew The River well.

Gabriel kept fighting against the current anyway, which was his natural impulse.

"Gabriel! Relax! Just let it take you!" Tabitha spoke more forcefully this time.

This time, he listened to her command. He turned onto his back and floated downstream. In a firm and steady way, the current moved him over some dips in the riverbed and guided him right to the middle of The River, where he was delivered into a calm eddy. The water was shallow enough for him to stand up again.

With a slight grin, he gave a reassuring wave of his arm to everyone standing on The Beach. Then he looked at a crook on the beachside of the rock and couldn't believe his eyes. There was a marble . . . his marble . . . the distinctive blue-and-gray Aggie. Gabriel pulled himself onto the rock and grasped the shiny marble. He laughed to himself as he held the sparkling treasure.

"I found my marble," he mumbled. "Hey, look. I found my marble! I found it!" he shouted back to everyone through his laughter.

"Looks more like he lost his marbles to me," Cig said, causing a few chuckles.

Stink raised his hand to Gabriel. "Wait there! We'll throw you a rope. You don't want to end up in the falls."

Stink ran to the van to retrieve the rope, and when he returned, he and several guys pulled Gabriel through the water and back to shore.

———————⬥———————

After they finished eating a pot of "hobo stew," as Jimmy called it, they sat around the fire, drinking hot chocolate and exchanging stories from the day. Rollie had already found a girl to befriend. She was giggling and pawing at his arm with each comment he made. Cig had a little too much Ripple, so he retired early.

"Ladies, I'm headed to my palace o' love if any of you would care to join me," he slurred.

"That's awfully nice of you, Cig," said one girl with tons of sarcasm.

"Maybe next time," chimed another.

With Cig slinking off to his tent, Jimmy made everyone laugh with his imitation of Stink jumping off the cliff earlier that day.

"Stevie looked like a giant stick man fighting his way through a spider web," he said. Then Jimmy flailed his arms in a pantomime motion.

One by one, they trailed off to bed until it was just Gabriel

and Tabitha sitting on opposite sides of the fire. Tabitha looked peacefully into the coals, the orange glow of the flames illuminating her face. Gabriel tried not to stare at her beauty, but he couldn't help it.

"I don't bite, you know." Tabitha continued to stare into the fire.

Gabriel wasn't sure what to say or do.

"I'll go get another log," he replied nervously.

He came back and sat down beside her and gently laid the log down on the hot coals. A beautiful upward shower of sparks floated toward the sky. After a few moments, he spoke up.

"How did you know about The River today? You know, when you told me to relax and let go."

"This isn't my first time here. I live pretty close by. I've run The River all over this canyon. My dad actually runs a rafting camp nearby. Most people want to fight The River instead of trust it. It's not what comes natural, but it's always what's best."

"The strength of the current took me by surprise. I was so focused on getting to that rock that I didn't really think about it."

"Yeah, what's the story about that marble anyway?"

"I like to collect marbles. I know it's stupid, but it's something I've done since I was a kid. My dad used to play marbles with me."

"I don't think it's stupid if it's something you love." Tabitha leaned over and rested her head on Gabriel's shoulder. His heart pounded with excitement. As he turned and looked down, her soft hair pushed against his cheek. She smelled so good . . . like flowers . . . or strawberries. The moment ended quickly as she picked her head up.

"Hey, you're going tomorrow right?"

"What's happening tomorrow? Jimmy never tells me anything. This whole trip has been a bit of a surprise." He paused for a moment. "A pretty amazing surprise so far."

Tabitha nudged closer. "Tomorrow, we're rafting the Big Water. It's going to be amazing. Trust me. I've run this portion of The River dozens of times. You can't even imagine what a rush it is. To feel the power and the speed of the water as it lifts you through the canyon . . . the waterfalls . . . the beauty of the landscape . . . and the drenching waves as they crash over you."

Tabitha had spoken dramatically and passionately. "I let you off the hook today, but you *have* to come with me tomorrow."

Gabriel considered her request. "Actually, I've never done anything like that before. Going on a river run sounds a bit out of my league." He could feel those butterflies in his stomach again.

"You can do it. You can't fully experience The River from the banks, Gabriel. You have to get in . . . all the way in."

Before he could respond, Tabitha stood up, dusted off the back of her pants, and adjusted the shawl draped over her shoulders. She took a deep breath through her nose and let it out.

"I love coming to The River."

She leaned closer, and her hair fell down onto his neck.

"Tomorrow is going to change your life," she whispered in a flirtatious tone.

He could feel her breath in his ear. He didn't dare move.

She turned and walked toward her tent. Looking back over her shoulder, she signed off for the night.

"Goodnight, Gabriel Clarke."

SAMUEL AND
BIG WATER ADVENTURES

Morning broke with a warming glow filling the canyon. Most of the camp started to stir before 8 a.m. in anticipation of their big day.

Around the breakfast campfire, those who'd done it before said that running The River through Whitefire Canyon would be the highlight of the trip. The veterans said this year would be an especially good run because an unusually warm and early spring had melted the winter snowpack and produced very high water.

High water meant fast water, they said. Some obstacles in The River would be easier to maneuver, but many others would be more difficult due to the speed of the water.

Gabriel listened, not saying much. He was excited and scared all at the same time.

After a Cig-cooked breakfast of bacon and eggs, Jimmy

announced they were rolling out in fifteen minutes.

"We've got to meet Samuel and everyone else at the put-in at 8:45 sharp," he said loudly. Jimmy always kept everyone on schedule.

Gabriel thought of all the excuses that would get him out of this river rafting experience. He knew he had none, but he wanted to be with Tabitha anyway. She had already informed him she wasn't taking no for an answer. The time had arrived to get past his fear. It was time to really live.

They packed their things and zipped up the tents so the animals wouldn't get to their food. Gabriel sat in the front passenger seat of Jimmy's van, staring at the rubber floor mat, trying to psych himself up for what lay ahead. On the way to her van, Tabitha tapped on his window.

Gabriel looked up to see her smiling face and quickly rolled down the window.

Tabitha reached in and grabbed his forearm, giving it a shake. "You ready for this?"

"Ready as I'll ever be." Gabriel issued a half-cocked grin, shaking his head as if to say, *I can't believe I'm doing this.*

"It's gonna be *awesome!*" Tabitha's eyes opened as wide as possible.

The vans rumbled along the state highway for a half hour until they got to their turn-off. Jimmy told the others that he knew exactly where they were going because he'd made the trip two years ago.

"Gabriel, you're going to love this, bro. I'm telling you, the first time I rafted Whitefire, it changed my life, man. You're going to wet your pants. It's just that much fun."

"Nice," Gabriel replied. "At least my pants will be warm. That water is seriously cold."

Jimmy laughed. "So what about Tabitha, huh? Huh?" He punched Gabriel in the arm. "Man, is she sweet on you or what?"

Gabriel couldn't contain his smile. "I'm not sure why she's hanging out with me, but I'm not complaining."

"She knows these waters like the back of her hand. She could actually guide one of these boats if she wanted to. She's been around The River all her life."

"Yeah, that's what she told me. She's really something."

"Here we are folks!" Jimmy made the last turn down a narrow gravel road to the put-in. This is where the boats would launch for the all-day excursion through Whitefire Canyon.

They all got out and stretched their legs while they took in the view. The River, which was maybe one hundred feet wide with a slight current, looked harmless. The vista was memorable, though, because of the way the sun's rays blasted through the treetops, illuminating the flow.

As they made their way to the water's edge, Gabriel found himself getting more and more nervous. He was imagining everything that could go wrong. He knew that once they shoved off, there was no turning back.

Five pale yellow rafts were sitting in the dirt near the water's edge. On one side of each raft were the faded words *Big Water Adventures* in white-stenciled lettering. The other side said *John's Whitewater Exp.* The guides were talking among

themselves and completing the necessary paperwork. When they were finished, they walked over toward the campers with clipboards in hand. One guy was obviously the leader.

"How's everyone doing today?" The lead guide sounded a bit like a college football coach with his husky voice.

"We're ready, baby!" Stink thrust an arm in the air as others whooped and hollered in agreement.

"Yeah, let's do this!" Cig chanted.

"Now that's what I like to see—an enthusiastic bunch!" The lead guide grinned, looking around at the other guides.

"It's going to be big water today, folks. Seriously big. You're in for a ride of a lifetime. Everyone has prepaid, so I just need everyone to sign the waiver before we launch. It's standard stuff. It just says you're running The River at your own risk and you realize that this is a dangerous activity." He began passing out these clipboards with the waivers.

"After you're done signing, join me over at that flat rock. We'll get you together with your guide, get your safety gear, do a little safety talk, and then you can hit The River."

The campers huddled around the guides and waited for their turn to sign their lives away.

"Anxious?" Tabitha came up beside Gabriel.

Gabriel hoped that she couldn't see the fear in his eyes.

"I've never done anything like this before."

"I was nervous my first time—and I grew up here. But once you get into the boat and hit the first rapid, you'll find your courage. Its like The River gives it to you *after* you take the first step, but a lot of people don't know that because they never get in the boat. If you don't get in, you'll never know what you're missing."

Tabitha quickly changed gears. "Hey, Samuel! I want you to meet somebody." She pulled Gabriel over to where the guide was standing and introduced him as the most experienced guide on The River. "Samuel's nickname is Kennedy because he bears a resemblance to the family," Tabitha said.

"Let's not start telling stories," the guide said.

"I promise not to. Anyway, Gabriel is a first timer. He'll be riding in our raft."

We're going to be in the same raft? Gabriel's heart leaped at the news.

The guide smiled. "Great, man. You're going to have a blast. It looks like our boat is made up of experienced rafters, so this is what I call an 'Allstate ride.' You'll be in good hands. I've got a pretty good track record."

Samuel looked to be a serious-minded guy in his mid-thirties. He was about five feet, ten inches tall and built like a welterweight boxer. Not an ounce of fat was on him. He had short, dark brown wavy hair with a little bit of gray at the temples and a scruffy beard.

"Welcome to The River, Gabriel. I better finish getting everyone paired up with their guides."

They announced the teams, and each of the rafters gathered around their respective guides. Tabitha, Gabriel, Stink, Jimmy, and Samuel would be rafting together. Samuel led everyone to a company van, which was hooked up to a box trailer that carried their safety gear.

"Go ahead and find a PFD that fits you as well as a brain bucket."

"PFD and a brain bucket?" Gabriel said.

"For you rookies, that's a Personal Flotation Device and a helmet. Pick up a paddle, too. This isn't a pleasure cruise. You're gonna have to work a little." To Gabriel's ears, it seemed that Samuel enjoyed that part of the speech.

"Once we get going, we've got about a thirty-minute float before the action begins, so I'll do our big safety talk on the water."

Tabitha came over to Gabriel as he was putting his life vest on and helped him cinch the straps tight. Then she grabbed the top of his vest on each side and pulled hard a couple of times. Her close proximity thrilled him.

"Gotta make sure it's tight enough in case someone has to pull you out of the water."

Samuel was directing traffic. "Hey, Gabriel, you look like a strong guy. Let's have you and Jimmy in the front of the boat. I'll explain why that's important in a few minutes."

Following Samuel's prompt, their group dragged the raft off the bank and into the water. They each gingerly waded into the cold water and then climbed in.

Gabriel's heart raced from the excitement. He reminded himself to take slow, deep breaths to help him stay calm as he sat down on his side of the raft. He looked for a place to hold, but there wasn't one. Samuel pushed the boat from shore and jumped in. They were the first boat in the water.

"Raise your paddles, guys!" Samuel lifted his paddle over

the boat and everyone joined in.

"To The River and a great run!" They brought their paddles together, forming a crest in the air.

"Woo-hoo! Here we go!" Tabitha yelled. She was sitting directly behind Gabriel.

As the boat drifted slowly down The River, Samuel began his safety talk.

"First off, let me say that I don't plan on losing anyone. "I've gone forty-eight runs without a swimmer, and I don't intend to start today. It's imperative that you stay in the boat, and there are three ways to do that. Number one: wedge your foot underneath the tube in front of you. You'll find a small strap on the bottom of the boat that you can slide your foot into for leverage. Number two: keep your entire paddle engaged in the water, not the tip of it. The whole blade pushes against the water and keeps you in the raft when we're engaging big water. Number three and more rare: I may call for you to move 'All in,' which means you get off the edge and sit on the floor of the raft, putting your paddles straight in the air. It's very important to get to the bottom of the raft immediately when I give you that command."

Gabriel had no trouble with that. He listened as Samuel discussed other commands like "Right forward hard," "Left forward hard," and "Swimmer," but their guide reiterated that he didn't want any swimmers on his watch. They practiced different levels of paddling and spinning the direction of the boat. With each term and technique, Gabriel gained confidence.

The tutorial continued as they moved listlessly down the

placid river. Samuel talked about the danger of "strainers"—obstacles such as branches and logjams where water can pass through but objects can't.

"You can get swept underneath these fairly easily, so if you're in the water, swim toward the strainer and explode out of the water as high as you can onto the strainer until you can be rescued."

They talked about hydraulics, boils, and suckholes. "When the water pours down into a crack in the riverbed, the water pours back over on itself, creating a huge tidal wave and suction to the bottom."

Gabriel digested everything that he was hearing. He felt like he was listening intensely.

"If for some reason you become a swimmer at one of the large falls or suckholes, and you're underwater and being tumbled around like you're in a washing machine, don't panic. Grab your paddle with both hands and raise it as high as you can out of the water. We'll see your paddle and pull you out. Ninety-nine times out of one hundred, if someone gets into trouble, it's because he or she panicked, fought the current, and got exhausted. If you're in that situation, just let The River take you. Point your feet downstream, and we'll come get you. Any questions?"

Gabriel could have asked a million, but he was trying to remember everything he had heard in the twenty-minute talk.

Samuel placed his paddle across his knees. "Go ahead and rest. In a few minutes, up around that corner, is our first set of rapids. That'll be a good warm-up for the day."

The water was moving gently as they coasted through the sandstone canyon. Gabriel took in the beauty of natural surroundings. This was a different perspective—a beautiful perspective—being on The River and seeing both banks, the eye-popping cliffs, the towering trees, and the large boulders that had tumbled down the mountain and were jutting out of the water. The vista was truly magnificent, and the view from The River was so much more visceral and complete.

As their raft got closer to the first bend, Gabriel could feel the pace of the water pick up. It was eerie and exciting to hear the sound of the rapids approaching but not see anything.

"Okay, guys, go ahead and get locked in. We're gonna want to hit this first set of rapids to the left of the giant rock. You can't miss it. Here we go. Forward hard!"

After Samuel gave the first command, just as they started to round the bend, they heard a loud shriek that echoed throughout the canyon. Gabriel had heard that sound before. He looked up and saw the majestic and mysterious white hawk circling over the canyon, like it was watching him.

The first rapids were approaching. Gabriel felt the ripple of the stronger current slapping the bottom of the raft as they picked up speed. The power of the water under their raft was amazing.

"Forward hard! Dig in!"

Samuel's command pulled everyone together in harmony as they hit the first rapid, just missing the big rock by only a foot or two. Down and up they splashed as the water sprayed up over the front of the raft. They hit four good-sized rapids in a row. Every time they pulled through a wave, Gabriel could feel the weight and power of the water. A wave would try to stop them, but the current and their rowing would push them through. Gabriel's eyes were wide open, and his heart pounded from the frigid water and the adrenaline pumping through his body.

"Good job, guys. You just made it through some Class II and III rapids there. A good warm-up for the Class IVs and Vs we'll hit later on!

I'm alive! I made it! This is truly amazing. I can't wait for the next rapid. Bring it on!

Gabriel loved the idea that he was really doing this—rafting on The River. This would never happen in Kansas.

"You mean we'll hit bigger water than that?" Gabriel asked.

"Oh, yeah. The River has a little more in store for us today." Samuel lifted his paddle out of the water. "Just take it as it comes and enjoy each moment. No two rapids are the same. That's what makes running The River so incredible. The River doesn't play all her cards at once, so we have to learn to stay close and listen well to what she's saying."

Gabriel was still nervous about what the day would hold, but as they would say, he was along for the ride. With each new rapid, he found his courage. Like a child taking his first steps and discovering what he's actually capable of, Gabriel was waking up to a new reality. With each passing moment, he wanted everything The River had to offer.

He was beginning to understand why his dad used to say, "We Clarkes—we're made for The River."

CHAPTER 14

CLASS V

The morning run on The River was fun and harrowing. Some of the rafters were banged up a bit, though. One young lady from another raft got knocked out from a big wave and was bloodied when she was struck by her own paddle.

Up until the lunch break, everyone in Samuel's raft stayed in. They were having the time of their lives. With every conquered rapid, Gabriel became more alive, more excited, and more confident. He was really glad he was on The River.

Many of the rapids, he learned, were named for various reasons. Rainbow Falls, for instance, was aptly named because of the rainbows that showed up in the spray when the water pounded the rocks. Most mornings, the sun came through the canyon at just the right angle and created a beautiful prism on The River's mist.

The Juicer was another amusing rapid. A deep crack in the

riverbed resulted in a massive wave and suckhole. The Juicer wasn't too difficult to navigate, but if a raft didn't enter with the correct amount of speed, the powerful currents folded the raft in half and "juiced" the riders right out of the boat.

Corkscrew, on the other hand, was very technical. Guides had to make sure they zigzagged back and forth across The River to avoid huge boulders that could pin them and create problems.

Thanks to Samuel's years of experience on The River, their raft successfully negotiated Rainbow Falls, The Juicer, and Corkscrew. Their on-the-river experience that morning could not have gone better for the rafters—especially for Gabriel. As they pulled to shore for their noontime break, Samuel informed them that there were two more major rapids left on the trip. "They're doozies," he said. "But then again, The River has saved the best for last."

They stopped for lunch at Mansion Turn, which turned out to be a welcome respite from their rigorous morning workout. Mansion Turn was a splendid section of The River where the gradient was almost level. On the right side was a small beach where there was room for the rafts to pull in. Mansion Turn— named for the towering columns of rock—was a popular place to have lunch, take a swim, or even hike up about forty feet to a small stoop and jump into a deep pool.

Twenty minutes after eating trail mix and apples, Samuel whistled. "Everybody gather around, please. We need to go over a few things before we finish the last leg."

Some were swimming in the calm eddy, while others were

still snacking. When everyone had congregated around the rafts resting on the shoreline, Samuel announced,

"We're going to leave in about fifteen minutes. This last section of The River is by far the most dangerous, but it's also the most fun. About a half-mile around the bend, we're going to hit two rapids back to back. The first one is called The Chutes. The gradient gets steep, so the water will be moving fast. The canyon walls come together and make a narrow passage where the water is squeezed through. Be ready because we'll be moving very quickly." He motioned with his hands as he spoke.

"If we hit The Chutes sideways, you'll get flipped over, and trust me, you don't want to ride The Chutes outside the boat. The bottom is full of huge boulders and rocks, which *would* ruin your day. Immediately following The Chutes, we barely have time to catch our breath before we hit Widowmaker Falls."

All chitchatting ceased. No one let out a peep. Everyone was listening with full intensity to what Samuel was saying.

"I don't tell you this to scare you, but you need to know that it's imperative to listen to your guide's every command. A man died at Widowmaker last week. No joke. He fell out on the first big drop and didn't follow his training. He tried to swim his way out of a huge hydraulic, but he panicked and wore himself out before we could get to him. He got sucked under, and that was the last we saw of him."

Gabriel got a knot in his stomach. The tone of the day was suddenly much more serious. The stakes had been raised.

"Here's the deal, guys." Samuel made eye contact with

several rafters. "I've done Widowmaker hundreds of times. It is a truly awesome section of The River, but it deserves our respect. We can and will do it safely, but we will treat it with respect and we will have a blast doing it. Everyone all right with that?"

"Let's do this!" Jimmy yelled from the back.

The meeting broke up, and everyone headed to their rafts. Gabriel felt like he had made so much progress. His belief in himself and The River had grown with each passing minute.

Samuel's pep talk jolted him to his core. He couldn't help but think about his father after hearing about Widowmaker. He'd played the scene of that fateful day over and over in his mind, countless times.

What if something like that happens to me? Is this really worth it?

Before he could sink deeper into worry, Tabitha grabbed his arm.

"Hey!" Tabitha said with hushed excitement. "We have a few minutes before we push off. Come with me!" She grabbed Gabriel by the elbow and started to walk.

"Where are we going?"

"You'll see. Just follow me."

Kicking pebbles underneath their feet, they climbed some rocks and hit some woods before coming upon a vista that overlooked The River.

"Wow, this is a beautiful view." Gabriel was a bit out of breath from the quick and vigorous climb.

"You want to go first or me?" Tabitha gestured toward the

still pools below, which had to be a good forty feet down.

"What?"

"We could go together!"

It finally dawned on Gabriel what Tabitha was saying.

"Jump? From here? We must be four stories up!"

"Come on. It'll be fun. I've done it tons of times."

Before Gabriel could even respond, Tabitha pecked his cheek with a kiss, grabbed his hand, and shouted, "One . . . two . . . three!"

Before he knew what was happening, he followed her and stepped into the abyss. They were airborne. Gabriel hung on to Tabitha's hand as long as he could, then let go. He involuntarily flailed his arms—because The River was still a long ways down.

"WHOA!"

He closed his eyes and braced for a feet-first landing. With a sizeable splash, he spilled into the chilly water but immediately surfaced like a submerged beach ball, thanks to the PFD around his chest.

When he got to the surface, his first thought was to find Tabitha. There she was! She was laughing her head off, and he swam to her and gave her a huge hug.

"That was so awesome!" he yelled. "Oh, man!"

Gabriel wiped his face with his hands and pushed his wet hair back. "I would have never done that on my own."

The kiss made it all possible.

He dragged himself to shore, and his buddies were saying things like, "What got into you?"

Gabriel didn't have an answer, but he did know that his fear of the future had faded a great deal. He could—and would—handle anything The River would throw at him.

———————

Like the calm before a big storm, they floated through the beautiful canyon, preparing for the most amazing whitewater that lay ahead at Widowmaker. Gabriel broke the silence and turned back to Tabitha.

"I'm going to get you for that," he vowed. "I don't know how, but it's coming!"

"We'll see about that," Tabitha laughed. "I wish I had a picture of that look on your face! See, you weren't even thinking about Widowmaker when you jumped. You were just living!"

"You suckered me, and you know it."

"Sure did."

Gabriel made a funny face, but he didn't mind . . . at all.

Samuel's voice brought him into the present. "Okay guys, let's get set. In about two minutes, you're about to start the ride of your lives."

Samuel got everyone focused. At this point, Gabriel thought, he was as ready as he'd ever be. The pace of the water accelerated, and he could hear the roar of the rapids just around the corner. They floated through the bend as Samuel guided the boat, using his paddle as a rudder. The decibel level rose exponentially from the crashing white water ahead.

As he was getting his bearings, Gabriel looked up and saw

the great white hawk circling over the rapids downstream. Then he turned, and they were arriving at the entrance of The Chutes. His fear faded into pure joy as he felt the raft move into the rapids and go up, then down . . . then up, then down . . .

"Forward hard!" Samuel shouted in the distance.

Water splashed from every side and tossed the boat around like a cork in a washing machine. Gabriel had a huge smile because he was having the time of his life. He whooped and hollered through the rapids as the raft dodged rocks and careened through the gorge. Each time a wave crashed over the bow, Gabriel accepted the fury of the water and just kept paddling. Everyone on the raft was yelling like teenage girls on a roller coaster.

They came through The Chutes perfectly.

As Gabriel caught his breath, he noticed that Samuel was still focused and intense.

"Okay . . . excellent, guys! Yes! You've got about sixty seconds to rest, and then we hit Widowmaker!"

Samuel steered the raft so that they were floating backward down The River. This would give them the right angle on Widowmaker, he explained.

"Stay focused! Right forward hard!"

This maneuver spun the boat around so they were facing downstream again. Gabriel looked ahead and saw a massive boulder in the middle of The River, and to the left of the boulder, a big drop-off, followed by another one where the horizon disappeared.

Samuel shouted several commands, and everyone followed

in perfect coordination. They hit the first drop dead on and powered through at breakneck speed. Then a massive wave poured over the front of the boat, drenching everyone. Like a writhing mechanical bull, the raft bucked through the massive somersault waves, grazing rocks below the surface.

Then the last drop came—Widowmaker Falls. Before Samuel could say anything, the right side of the raft overpowered the left side—and the raft turned slightly to the left. Samuel yelled for a correction, but they hurtled over the last drop . . . sideways.

The yellow raft hit the bottom of the falls, and a brick wall of water smacked them violently. Like a killer whale tossing a sea lion in a vicious attack, The River threw the helpless raft straight up in the air, which catapulted everyone into the churning water.

Arms and legs thrashing, the rafters were scattered in the boiling waters. Within seconds, Samuel bounced back up and grabbed on to the raft, which was drifting downstream upside down. One by one the rafters surfaced, all except Gabriel. The current slowed a hundred yards downstream, and Stevie and Samuel pulled the raft over to the right side.

"Anybody see Gabriel?" Jimmy shouted.

Tabitha was on the other side of The River, catching her breath in a waist-deep eddy. As they were all looking around frantically, he popped up from underneath the white water and started floating toward the others. Clutching his paddle, Gabriel aimed his feet downstream and floated until the water slowed and he could get his feet under him.

Everyone cheered his arrival.

"You okay?" Jimmy shouted.

Gabriel found himself in water shallow enough to stand up in. He put his hands over his face, took a deep breath, and slammed his paddle into the water like he was chopping wood—because he was happy. Then, reminiscent of a medieval warrior with a spear in hand, he hoisted his paddle high over his head, over and over.

"YEAHHHHHHHHHH! I did it! I did it! Yes! Woo-hoo!" Gabriel shook the canyon with his battle cry. His fear and indifference had been shattered—forever.

The River had opened up a whole new world to him.

A world he was destined for.

He was sure that his life would never be the same.

CHAPTER 15

The Last Night

On the last night before the trip back to Kansas, all the campers sat around the campfire, reliving the amazing experience they had on The River that day. Most were exhausted and ready to go home. Others, like Gabriel, just wanted to stay.

His day of river-rafting had taken him to another world. The River had captured Gabriel in a special way, and he wasn't alone.

"Did you see how high Stink flew out of the boat at Widowmaker?" Jimmy slapped his thigh in laughter.

"Apollo 11 to the moon," said Rollie. "We're talking sky high."

Stink quietly stood up and took a gangly butler's bow. "At your service," he quipped, and everyone laughed some more. The conversations and story-swapping went on into the wee hours of the morning, their faces illuminated by the light of the fire.

By 2:30 a.m., all the tired campers had finally turned in . . . except for Gabriel. His head was spinning from everything he had experienced in a few short days. His body was numb with fatigue, but his mind raced. He got up and moved to an old log next to The River. He thought about the stirring of the water and the white red-tailed hawk . . . the healing encounter as well as the vivid memories he made on The River. Jumping off the rock at Mansion Turn with the girl who had stolen his heart, as well as riding the big water, had opened up a whole new world for him.

Nothing compares to what I've experienced here. How can I go back to my dead-end job after this?

"How come you aren't asleep yet? Aren't you exhausted?" Tabitha put her hand on his shoulder as she sat down on the log beside him. Gabriel thought she had gone to sleep in her tent. He was thankful she hadn't.

"I just can't shut my mind down. We don't have much time left before we leave in the morning, and I want to take it in a little more."

"That's why I've stayed here . . . near The River. It's all I know. It's all I *want* to know really. I never get bored here." Tabitha stared ahead dreamily. "There's always a new adventure, something exciting around the next corner. I'm sure I'll see other places, but I'll always want to be with The River, wherever I go."

Tabitha spoke passionately. After a few moments of silence,

she moved down to the sand in front of him. She lay back on the beach and looked up at the stars.

"Come down here." She patted the sand next to her. Gabriel didn't waste any time. He laid down next to her and looked up at the starlit canvas above.

"It's so clear tonight," Tabitha said. "Doesn't it look like there's some sort of powerful light behind the night sky, like God poked holes in the darkness to give us a small glimpse of what's on the other side?"

"You see things in such a unique way . . . like no one I've ever known."

"Really? Maybe it's because most people don't take time to really *see* what's all around them. My mother told me that when I was five years old, I'd walk around holding a pretend camera and take pictures of everything I thought was beautiful. She told me I'd say, 'I don't want to forget anything, so I'm taking pictures.' I guess I've really never stopped doing that in a sense. The older you get, though, the easier it is to forget to use the 'camera.' "

"Wow. That's amazing. I think I've spent most of my life staring at mental pictures of the past. They weren't good pictures, so maybe I've missed some stuff along the way."

"I think all of us are guilty of that. My mother had a little poem she used to recite, and it goes like this:

Yesterday is gone and you can't change it.
There are no guarantees for tomorrow, so save it.
The best stuff is now, so live today and don't dare waste it."

"Your mother sounds like a pretty special lady."

"She was. I miss her a lot."

Gabriel wasn't sure what to say. After a few moments of silence, he asked her.

"She's gone?"

"Yeah. She lost her fight to cancer eight years ago. I was thirteen. She was the most amazing person I've ever known."

Gabriel's heart sank. He couldn't believe she had lost a parent, too.

Tabitha turned over and propped herself up on her elbows. She reached for a locket hanging around her neck and opened it.

"That's her." She held the gold locket up to Gabriel. He sat up and pulled the pendant in close.

"She's beautiful. You look just like her. What's her name?"

"Alaina—Alaina Fielding. Everybody called her Laney."

"What an interesting name . . . it suits her." Gabriel kept staring at the color picture, mesmerized by the striking resemblance between mother and daughter.

"Her mother—my grandmother—was French. Grandmère told me Alaina meant 'little rock.' My mom went through a lot even before her cancer, but she never broke. I think her name reflects her character."

"So what does Tabitha mean?"

"Oh, no. I was afraid you'd ask me that."

"Come on, tell me."

"All right, but don't laugh. It means . . . gazelle. I would have preferred something along the lines of 'noble princess' or 'goddess,' but hey, what can you do?" They both chuckled.

"I don't know. I think the name suits you. Gazelles are fast, graceful, and visually stunning." Gabriel couldn't believe he was being so bold.

Their conversation was interrupted by a strange sound. Tabitha put her hand over her mouth as she saw what it was.

"Oh. My. Gosh." Tabitha turned the other way.

Gabriel perked up and turned around toward the woods to see what was stirring.

"Are you kidding me?" Gabriel started laughing.

There was Cig, staggering and belching intermittently, taking a leak on a tree.

"Thank heaven it's dark," Tabitha remarked.

"Yeah, *nobody* needs to see that," Gabriel smirked. The two rolled back over on their backs and laughed hysterically.

After Cig retired to his quarters, Tabitha stood up.

"Come with me. I want to show you something."

Does this girl ever stop moving? Gabriel wondered.

He got up and brushed the sand off the back of his trousers.

"Here, turn around." Tabitha helped him with the sand on his backside. Then she grabbed his hand and took him upstream along the beach and into the woods.

"I can't see anything," Gabriel said.

"Just follow me." Tabitha spoke with confidence.

They carved their way through the woods by the light of the moon, dodging branches and stepping on fallen branches and twigs. After several minutes, they came to a large rock jutting out into the calm water. They both made their way out and sat on the rock, side by side, watching the moonlight reflect off the water with a soft glow.

"I can't believe this trip is over. I don't want it to end." Gabriel looked directly at Tabitha. "These have been an amazing few days."

"It doesn't have to end," she said tenderly.

"What do you mean?"

"I mean you could come back for the summer."

"I have a job in Kansas I have to get back to. My mom is there, and Mister Earl could use my help on the farm." Gabriel sounded forlorn and frustrated.

"We run a guide-mentoring program all summer long. You could come back and work with me. There's tons of stuff to do. The adventure camp is full of great people who have a terrific time all summer long. It doesn't pay much, but you'll be here, with me . . . at The River."

Gabriel was stunned by what he heard. Could this really be a possibility? He could be with Tabitha. But what would happen to his mom? How would Mister Earl survive without the extra hand on the farm? And he'd have to tell Mr. Baggers at the Five & Dime that he was quitting his job. His boss wouldn't like that. But he wanted to be with Tabitha. He wanted to be with The River.

His mind was in a tug of war. This was a huge crossroads in his life. The River had opened up a whole new world to him. Tabitha seemed too good to be true. A girl who saw past his insecurities and reached out to him with strength and grace.

Yet it was those same insecurities and self-doubt that rose to the surface once again.

"I don't know. You've been with me for only a few days. You may not want me around that much. Besides, I don't know anything about working at an adventure camp."

"Well . . . it's up to you . . . but I'm telling you, we would have so much fun. Don't you want to run The River again? There are so many parts of The River you haven't seen."

"I know. I'd love to run it again . . . and again. After today, I don't think I could ever get enough."

Tabitha looked deep within his eyes. "Don't you want to see me again?"

"Of course, I do." This time, Gabriel didn't hesitate to respond as he looked right back into her eyes. "It's just that . . ."

Before Gabriel could finish his sentence, she leaned in quickly and kissed him on the lips. Then again . . . longer this time. His heart pounded, and he felt his whole body flush with adrenaline. The way she smelled, the way she tasted. A girl had never kissed him like that before. He didn't know what to do. He was frozen. Tabitha leaned back over and pushed her hair behind her ears. The silence was deafening.

"I'm sorry . . . I just thought . . ." Tabitha couldn't finish her sentence. "Goodnight, Gabriel."

She got up and started to leave.

"Wait!"

She kept walking.

"Tabitha . . . please. I can explain everything."

She paused for a moment and looked back. Her eyes were

red and watery.

"Good night," she said with disappointment.

What did I do? It all happened so fast.

By now, it was four o'clock in the morning. Gabriel sat on the rock, bewildered at what had happened. He had dreamed of a girl like her and a kiss like that. Then he played over and over in his mind why things had ended on such a bad note. He thought about her offer and whether Kansas was still the place for him.

He was still thinking when the sun came up.

A cloud cover and light rain moved into the canyon as they began packing up their tents and gathering their belongings. The cool drizzle seemed to symbolize the sadness of having to leave The River. Jimmy didn't waste anytime corralling his guys to get loaded up and on the road.

"Okay, I think that about does it. Stink, did you get all our pots and pans?"

"Affirmative, sir," Stink saluted.

Rollie finished saying goodbye to one of the chiquitas he had met on the trip. Their heads looked like they were joined together at the mouth. Cig was in the front seat, leaning back with his hands on his head, moaning from tying one on the night before. Jimmy got in the driver's seat and slammed the door.

"Ouch! Not so hard, man. My brain is hurting."

"What's the matter, Cig? A little tender this morning?"

Stink leaned out the side door of the van.

"Gabriel! Let's go, man!" He turned to the others. "What's he doing? Does he not realize it's raining?"

Gabriel was standing at the water's edge, staring out over The River. He turned around slowly, pulled the hood of his sweatshirt over his head, and made his way back, looking around The Beach for any sign of Tabitha. His heart was heavy.

Surely, he would get to say goodbye, but there was no sign of her anywhere. Maybe she had left with one of the first cars when he wasn't looking. Glancing around the beach one last time, he turned and climbed into Jimmy's van and shut the door.

Jimmy started the van and put it into gear. "Back to Kansas, boys."

Just as he began to pull out, they heard a banging on the side door.

"Hey! Hold up!" Tabitha shouted.

Gabriel was thrilled to see her. Jimmy stopped the van.

"You can't leave without saying goodbye," she said. Gabriel could barely hear her through the closed window because the rain had begun to pick up. He opened the door and hopped out.

"I didn't know where you were," he said. Then he realized all the guys were sitting quietly and watching the encounter.

"Guys, can you give me a minute?" Gabriel asked. He steered Tabitha away from the van.

"I'm sorry about last night. I just . . ."

"It's okay. But you have to come back, Gabriel. My offer still stands. Come spend the summer with me at The River. Guide Camp starts in two weeks. You won't regret it." The rain was dripping down her face.

Tabitha lunged into his arms, and they embraced for several moments, oblivious to the deluge.

After saying goodbye, he wondered if Tabitha . . . and The River . . . were seeing the last of Gabriel Clarke.

He had some big decisions to make.

CHAPTER 16

❧ Goodbye and the Journal ❧

"Gabriel! What are you doing? I need those soda cases stacked before you get out of here!"

Gabriel knew his daydreaming was a source of frustration for Mister Baggers. Ever since his arrival back in Cairo a couple of days earlier, he had trouble kicking it into gear at the Five & Dime. Summer was coming on strong, and he had only a few days to decide what he was going to do about Tabitha's invitation.

He missed his new friend terribly, but he hadn't summoned the courage to call her. There was so much to consider, which was driving him crazy. Furthermore, he couldn't get out of his mind the memories of his trip to The River. At home, he found himself staring at Miss Collingsworth's painting and mentally re-enacting those amazing days on and off the water.

Returning to his old life wasn't holding much appeal.

Everything was different. He'd experienced something greater than himself, and he wanted more. This was his destiny. His father's words echoed in his ears: *We Clarkes, we were made for The River.*

But something was keeping him from taking that step of faith.

"Did you hear me? Are all the sodas packed away?"

Gabriel interrupted his reverie. "All done, Mister B. Can I go now?"

"I guess so."

Gabriel got into his old Ford step-side and headed back to the farm on a warm, lazy Thursday evening in Cairo. He pulled up to the barn where he usually parked his truck. He stepped out and whistled for Rio. Usually his faithful dog ran to meet him at the front of the property, but the last few days he'd been a little slow. Rio loped around the back of the barn with his tongue hanging out.

"Hey, buddy. You feeling all right?" Gabriel knelt down and grabbed him from behind both ears and scratched his head. Rio perked up a bit but still seemed lethargic.

"He might have eaten something he shouldn't. He's done that before." Mister Earl showed up from behind the barn as well.

"He sure doesn't seem like himself."

"Well, he is gettin' up in years. Who knows exactly how old he is."

"Dinner's on!" Miss Vonda squawked from the front porch.

"That woman's voice carries to the next county." Mister

Earl shook his head.

Gabriel chuckled. "We better get in there."

———————◆◆◆———————

One of the bright spots of living on the farm was sharing a meal as well as Miss Vonda's cooking together. Tonight, dinner was one of Maggie's favorites—buttermilk fried chicken and biscuits. Miss Vonda always prepared fresh green beans cooked with bacon and some kind of pie for dessert with this meal.

Maggie was helping set the dining room table when both men arrived. "Did you gentleman wash up?" she asked as she put the last two glasses of iced tea on the table.

"Yes, ma'am," the two answered in unison.

The four of them sat down at the painted white farm table. Mister Earl took off his John Deere hat and tossed it toward the sofa, the signal to bow their heads in concert as the older man said grace.

"Lord, we thank thee for this meal. May it nourish our bodies for thy service."

"Amen," they chimed together.

The Cartwrights weren't very religious, but they never missed thanking the Good Lord for His bounty and provision whenever they sat down together for a meal.

The sound of serving utensils clanging against the various plates of food filled the dining area. A few minutes into the meal, conversation finally broke out.

Miss Vonda was cutting in her leg of fried chicken when

she turned to Gabriel. "Tell us about your trip with those boys. We haven't seen much of ya, and we'd all like to know. You stayed out of trouble, didn't ya?"

"Yeah, honey. I'm dying to hear about it," Maggie chimed in. She sensed Gabriel's distance, but he seemed like he was in a good place, so she didn't want to push things.

"It was a good trip." Gabriel kept eating, but a huge smile took over his countenance. He couldn't contain his joy.

A mom's intuition told her there was more to be said. "You're not getting off that easy. Your face says it all. Come on! Tell us what happened." Maggie was excited to see him so happy.

"We camped . . . hiked a little . . . no big deal."

"You're hiding something. I know it!" Maggie kept at him as she buttered a biscuit. Mister Earl and Miss Vonda just listened.

"Okay! Okay! I met a girl. It's no big deal."

"If it's no big deal, then tell us about her."

Gabriel's face turned red from embarrassment. He sought to change the subject.

"I rafted the big water. That was huge. You can't imagine the canyons and beauty of The River. At first I didn't want to do it, but Tabitha convinced me to go . . . ."

"Tabitha . . . so that was her name, huh?" Maggie spoke with a jealous smile.

"We jumped together off of a forty-foot cliff into the water. She was in my raft. We went through Class V whitewater, which can be super dangerous. You should have seen Stink fly out of our raft. That was amazing." The sentences were gushing out of Gabriel's mouth. It was like he wasn't coming up for air.

Maggie couldn't believe what she was hearing. *My Gabriel? Making friends with a girl and rafting huge whitewater?*

"This girl *must* be something if she got you to do all of that!"

"It wasn't just Tabitha . . . even though she was definitely amazing. The River itself was spectacular. Like nothing I've ever experienced. I mean . . . there's too much to explain. I felt like I came alive or something."

Gabriel's passion escalated. "I had these moments where it was like The River spoke to me. I know it sounds weird." He shook his head. "To feel the thunder of that whitewater lift you through the canyon, and then fifteen minutes later swim in calm, swirling eddies . . . it's like no other place."

Then he remembered something else. "There was this beautiful white hawk with red tail feathers who kept showing up at different times. It was like the hawk was there just for me. I'm telling you, it was awesome."

Everyone was mesmerized by his speech.

"What else can you tell us?" his mother asked.

"I mean, it was like Dad was there with me, you know what I mean?" He took another bite of his chicken.

Maggie was speechless. Mister Earl and Miss Vonda just glanced at each other from across the table. Nobody knew what to say when he mentioned his father.

"That's great, honey." Maggie wasn't sure how to respond to this revelation.

"I want to go back," her son declared.

"Great idea. You should go back next year. Maybe it could become a tradition or something."

"No, I mean now. I want to go back now. I've been invited to go to work at a whitewater camp with Tabitha's father."

This news hit Maggie like a thunderbolt. Gabriel sounded as if his mind was made up. Her countenance dropped.

"What about your job? And what about the farm? Mister Earl might need . . . "

"I'll manage," Mister Earl interrupted.

"How long will you be gone?" she asked.

"Nearly four months. They need help from June through September. If I'm going to make it for the start, I need to leave Saturday."

"That's only two days away." Maggie was disheartened at the thought of Gabriel leaving. Since he came to live with her, he'd never gone away for any length of time.

Deep in her heart, though, she knew this could be a good opportunity for her boy, but she was worried. Worried that something bad might happen. Worried about him being at The River. Worried about what she'd do without him. He'd been her life for the last sixteen years.

"If you'll excuse me." Maggie set her napkin on the table and stood up.

"Is something wrong, Mom?"

Maggie hoped her disappointment didn't show. "I'm sorry—this all seems awfully sudden."

Miss Vonda spoke up. "I know exactly how you feel, dear."

Maggie sat back down reverently to hear what Miss Vonda had to say.

"It feels like your whole world gets turned upside down when your kids leave home," said the older woman. "Earl and I felt this way when our first boy said he wanted to join the Army right after Pearl Harbor. He was twenty at the time."

"He was a man. He needed to make his own decisions," Mister Earl said. "The River sounds like a pretty exciting place, if you ask me." Mister Earl looked at Gabriel with a slight grin as he went for seconds of chicken and beans. "Am I right?"

"Yes, sir. All I know is that I'm going nowhere fast here in Cairo. The River showed me there's so much more to experience out there. I don't want to miss it while stacking sodas with Mister Baggers."

Gabriel turned to his mother. "I'll come back, Mom. I grew up here. It's all I've known. But it's like The River is calling me, and I have to go."

Maggie's heart was stirred. Mister Earl was right—her son was a man now. He needed to follow his heart.

"I want you to be careful," she said.

"I will . . . you know I will."

After telling Mister Baggers it was his last day, Gabriel drove home and finished a few last-minute chores for Mister Earl.

It was past dusk. Now all he had left to do was pack up for

his trip. While hoisting a heavy cardboard box into the truck bed, he heard a whimper from Rio, who was lying down beside his front tire. Gabriel sat down beside him and stroked the thick fur of his neck.

"Well, buddy. This is it. I'm leaving tomorrow. But just for a little while. I'll be back before you know it."

Rio whimpered and nudged his head onto Gabriel's lap.

"I first met you at The River, didn't I? Yep, you saved my life. At some point, I want you to meet Tabitha. She's beautiful. I know she'd like you, too. I'll come back for you." Gabriel leaned down touched his forehead to Rio's. "I'm gonna miss you, boy."

"I'm gonna miss *you*." His mother's voice came out of nowhere. She stood next to the pickup truck, holding a small package.

"Thanks, Mom. I'm going to miss you, too. Don't worry. I'll be back soon."

Maggie strolled closer to Gabriel and Rio, her eyes moist and swollen.

"I've been waiting for the right time to give you this. I suppose now is as good a time as any." She handed Gabriel a large, flat, brown padded envelope with the end torn off. The creased envelope was stained from handling.

"What is it?" Gabriel stood up and dusted his jeans off.

"I found this in the pocket of my bag after I moved to Kansas. I never got the chance to give it back to him."

She began to tear up again. "When you told me you wanted to go back to The River, I knew you should have it. It's real special." She extended the package to him.

Gabriel reached inside the envelope and pulled out a leather-bound book. The lack of light made it too dark to read, so he opened up the truck door and turned his headlights on.

He walked around in front of the truck and held the book in front of the headlights, and dust particles danced in beams of light as Gabriel looked closer at the dark leather, antique-looking book. The cover was soft dark brown leather, scratched and stained. The pages were thick, like parchment. Gabriel opened up the cover, and the first page read: *The River Journal, 1931.* At the bottom of the page in handwritten script were the names *R. Allen Clarke* and in a different, darker ink, **John W. Clarke**.

"Is this Dad's journal?" Gabriel flipped through the pages and saw notes, diagrams, and hand-drawn pictures, as well as journal entries from decades before.

"It was your grandfather's when he was young. He passed it along to your father before he died. They talked about The Journal quite often. There was hardly ever a time that your dad didn't have this journal with him. I saw him reading and writing in this more times than I could count. Your father said it contained the ways of The River. 'Wisdom from decades of running The River and exploring the canyons are in this book,' he would say."

Gabriel sat speechless. He kept turning the pages slowly. The sound of his fingers against the rough pages was like a sacred moment to him. He read a few sentences underneath a hand-drawn picture of a rock formation with water pouring over and around it. The section said:

Today, I am once again in awe of The River. This large rock was not here yesterday. It fell in overnight due to the strength of the water loosening the dirt around it. Little by little, day-by-day, the rock will never be the same. The River is shaping everything in its path, including this rock. As the water collides with it, new and beautiful art is created. I want everyone to experience the " art " of The River.

R. Allen Clarke

Another entry read:

The River never sleeps. Always moving, relentless in pursuit of its destination. The River is alive.

R. Allen Clarke

About three-quarters of the way through the book, a beautiful charcoal sketch of a little boy caught his eye. His father had written this note next to it:

I cannot wait until Gabriel is old enough to enjoy this with me. He is already so strong

and feisty as a three year old. He has The
River in him. He has no fear. Today he said,
"Daddy, I'm gonna be stronger than you." I
believe he will be one day.

    J.W.C.

Gabriel closed the book gently and clutched it to his chest. He turned and looked at his mother. "Thank you," he whispered, holding out his arms. He and his mother embraced.

"Please be careful, Gabriel." His mother was unsuccessful at holding back her tears. "I just can't imagine . . ."

"Don't worry, Mom. I'll be back sooner than you think. I know this is what I'm supposed to do."

"I know. I know." She gave him one last hug and walked back toward the house.

"Mom?"

She turned around.

"The Journal . . . it makes me feel close to him."

She nodded and continued on.

Gabriel sat back down next to Rio, and by the glow of the truck headlights, began to thumb through more of The Journal. He connected with his past . . . and began to discover the possibilities of his future.

The sun had not yet risen, but the glow of its eminent arrival colored the sky. Mister Earl, Miss Vonda, and Maggie were all there to see him off. Mister Earl didn't say much. He just kept his hands in his coveralls pockets. Miss Vonda gave him a basket of goodies for the road. His mother wiped proud tears from her eyes.

They all knew this was the right trip for Gabriel . . . not easy, but right. After one last squeeze from his mother, Gabriel climbed in and started his truck. He rolled down his window.

"See you in September!" Gabriel waved his left arm out the window as he drove away. His new treasure, The Journal, sat on the seat next to him.

"I've got a feeling it's going to be longer than four months," Mister Earl said as he headed toward the barn.

CHAPTER 17

❧ NO MORE KANSAS ❧

Fourteen hours of driving alone, mostly on Highway 70 West, gave Gabriel plenty of time to meditate on what the journey to Big Water Adventure Camp meant for him. He certainly felt a newfound freedom once he had left Kansas behind in his rearview mirror. Like an eaglet leaving the nest perched high on a cliff to discover his wings, Gabriel jumped to freedom as well. Kansas had its good memories, but life there included a lot of heartache and loneliness.

Sure, he felt safe—even loved—in Cairo. The small town and childhood friends were all he had known for most of his life. In his heart, though, he knew that life had more in store for him. The trouble was that he just didn't know where to begin.

On his trip with Jimmy Bly and the guys just two weeks before, he had captured a glimpse of what life could be. Then receiving The Journal from his mother expanded—

no, exploded—his horizons. He recalled a quote from his grandfather that he read the night before: "Life is not to be merely survived—it is meant to be lived."

His grandfather's words from the past resonated with him to his core. Living . . . really living . . . was on Gabriel's mind now. He didn't know exactly what the future held for him during the next few months, but he was excited—excited to breathe the crisp mountain air, exhilarated to spend more time on The River, and thrilled to see Tabitha again.

Exhausted from his predawn to sundown excursion, Gabriel sipped the last few drops of his truck stop coffee before making the final turn. He was relieved yet a bit nervous to see the large weathered sign announcing Big Water Adventure Camp with a large painted finger telling him which way to go. Gabriel pulled into a large gravel cul-de-sac and parked his pickup truck next to the other vehicles. There were a couple of beat-up Chevrolet vans, several other dented pickups, and a couple of old jeeps that looked like they had crashed down the side of the mountain a time or two.

The cul-de-sac was surrounded by several wood cabins scattered around the property at different elevations on the mountainside. A large timber lodge, suitably rustic, sat directly on The River. Built into the side of the hill that sloped down to the water's edge, the timber lodge looked like it had undergone several additions over the years.

It was dusk, and the camp was eerily quiet. Gabriel saw a few lights on in the front office, so he headed in that direction.

As he approached a rickety screen door painted fire-engine

red, Gabriel could hear laughter and music playing, but the sounds were faint. He opened the screen door, but a little bell startled him as it jingled above his head. He walked in slowly as the creaking door slammed behind him.

There was no one in sight, but the rousing conversation continued in the distance. Gabriel craned his neck to determine where the merriment was coming from inside camp headquarters. Standing in the foyer, he saw a long counter in front of him. This was undoubtedly where folks checked in. The walls were littered with vintage rafting gear, tacked-up newspaper clippings, and hundreds of faded photos of people who had experienced The River. He was looking at some of the faces when one of the older newspaper articles caught his eye.

"Jacob Fielding Defies Odds" was the headline printed over a picture of a bearded man with a solemn look on his face. He had dark curly hair and was standing in The River, holding a paddle over his head. The article started out:

Jacob Fielding has become one of the most revered adventurers in the West. How did this happen?

It was a cool morning in 1955 when . . .

A door slammed, startling Gabriel. An older black man emerged from the back room, singing to himself in a deep, raspy tone a song that sounded like an old Negro spiritual to Gabriel's ears: "Hmmmmm . . . wade out in the water . . . Oh, oh . . . wade out in the water."

After a few seconds, he finally looked up and noticed Gabriel.

"Sorry 'bout that. Can I help you?" The short, bowlegged man moseyed to the counter and extended Gabriel a gentle smile. He seemed to be in his late sixties and couldn't have been much over five feet tall. With reading glasses hanging around his neck by a string, he had donned a tan fishing hat, tattered green cardigan sweater, and well-worn khaki workpants with boots. He held an old book in one hand and a pipe in the other as he waited for Gabriel's reply.

"I'm here to help out this summer. I'm Gabriel . . . Gabriel Clarke."

"Oh, yes. We were hoping you'd come." His voice was gravelly, and he squinted his eyes a bit as he looked at Gabriel and gestured with his pipe.

"Follow me, and I'll take you to the others. I'm just headed to my room for my evening read. A pipe, my rocker, and a good book—that's all I need every night."

The man kept talking as he pushed open the half-door that let Gabriel behind the counter. "I'm Ezra, by the way. Ezra Buchanan. If you ever need anything, just holler." They walked through a couple of doors and then down a flight of stairs that moaned with every step.

They were getting closer to the conversation and the music.

"Watch your head, son. This door frame is low for you tall people."

Gabriel's head just cleared as he made his way through the door at the bottom of the stairs. They walked in to find a dozen young people laughing and carrying on. They were snacking on corn chips and drinking soda. Over in one corner, one guy was strumming a ukulele. Gabriel felt much like he did on the first day of school. It was never easy being the new kid on the block. He quickly canvassed the room but there was no sign of her.

"Hey, kids. Got someone for you to meet."

"Ezra!" a few shouted, raising their soda bottles to him. Ezra took off his hat to reveal a crown of pure white, shortly cropped hair. He nodded to acknowledge the greeting.

"This here's Gabriel Clarke. He's going to be joining us for the summer, so make him feel welcome."

"Welcome to Big Water, man." A familiar face emerged from the kitchen. It was Samuel—his guide from two weeks earlier. Gabriel was relieved to see him. Samuel held out his hand, and Gabriel gave him a firm shake.

While they were exchanging pleasantries, Ezra tugged on Gabriel's sleeve. "Young man, I'm going to read some. My room is off the back of the rigging area. That's where we store the rafts. Actually, your room is right next door to mine. If you get lost, the others will know where it is. If you need anything, just stop by." Ezra excused himself out the back door.

One by one, each of the would-be guides introduced themselves to Gabriel.

"You vant something to drink?" one of the girls asked from behind the bar in the kitchen. She spoke with a Scandinavian accent.

Gabriel looked in her direction, and she held out her hand and gave Gabriel a surprisingly strong squeeze.

"My name is Stasia," she said. The young woman was short

and stocky with white-blonde cornsilk-like hair cut in a bob. She had very fair skin, rosy cheeks, and crystal blue eyes.

"Nice to meet you. Yeah, something to drink would be great. I'm thirsty after the long drive."

"You're the one from Kansas, right?"

"That's correct."

"You're training to be a guide, yeah?"

"Oh, no. I'm just here to help out and work around the camp for the summer. I just took my first raft trip a few weeks ago."

"I took my first trip down The River two years ago, and I haven't been able to leave the area since. It's magnificent around here. I guide whitewater in the summer, and I'm a ski instructor in the winter. There are several of us who do that."

Gabriel sat down and listened to snippets of conversations around the room. The energetic atmosphere lent itself to stories about trips they had taken earlier that day.

Cool and damp air breezed through the open windows. From this vantage point, Gabriel could hear The River bubbling in the background. As he looked around, though, he couldn't help but wonder where Tabitha was. He thought about asking someone if she had been around, but then Samuel stood up in front of the room.

"Okay, guys, if I could have your attention, please. Here are your assignments for the week. Part of your training is getting to know all of the duties involved in running a camp, not just the sexy part." He passed out the paperwork. Samuel sounded like a military officer. "That means kitchen duty, raft maintenance, trash duty—that sort of thing. This is an all-inclusive resort. You get included in everything."

They chuckled . . . nervously. Samuel looked toward Gabriel. "I'll get with you after the meeting to go over your specific duties."

Samuel finished passing out several sheets of paper and went over some particulars on each page. Gabriel zoned out and pondered what he had gotten himself into. He continued to wonder when he'd get to see Tabitha.

When the meeting was over, some of the others scattered to their cabins while a few stayed behind to chat or play cards.

"Gabriel, if you want to get your things, I'll meet you out in front of the office and show you where you're staying," Samuel offered.

"Okay, great." Gabriel made his way back up the stairs and out to his truck. He grabbed his duffel bag, slung it over his shoulder, and picked up one of the boxes with his stuff in it. Samuel came around the corner of the lodge.

"Let me help you with that." Samuel took the box and started to walk down the gravel drive past the lodge toward a large barn-like structure, down closer to The River. "You're going to be helping in various areas around the camp. I've got you working closely with Ezra. He manages the grounds and the equipment, as well as makes some mean cinnamon rolls. He's been here longer than anyone and will show you the ropes. It's pretty much seven days a week around here during the season, but you'll have some personal time to run the river, do some exploring, or whatever."

They made their way down around the back of the large barn building. They got on a well-worn mossy path that cut into the woods along The River. "Smell that? If you get lost, just follow the smell of Ezra's pipe." Sure enough, Gabriel took a big whiff and smelled the nutty pipe smoke.

"That smells good."

"Good thing you like it 'cause Ezra puffs on that thing a lot."

After a couple of minutes, they came upon the back of the small cabin just up the hill from the path. Ezra was seated in his rocking chair on the deck, puffing on his pipe, reading a book by the dim porch light. They walked up the slope, stepping on the rocks placed there for good footing.

"Come on in, gentlemen." Ezra stood up quickly and showed Gabriel to his room, which was adjacent to Ezra's. They shared a bathroom in between.

"I'll see you in the morning, Gabriel. We have breakfast in the kitchen at 8 a.m." Samuel put Gabriel's box down on the floor and excused himself quickly.

The cabin was primitive: a single bed, a plain night table, a lamp, and a small pine dresser. Gabriel didn't mind. That's about all he had back in Cairo. He opened the door to the deck and took in the view. The River was a stone's throw away and sounded like heaven as it rippled along. The glow of moonlight reflected off the water, and the unmistakable scent of pine and fir filled the forest. Further over on the deck, Ezra had returned to his rocking chair and his book.

Gabriel walked back into his bedroom to unpack his

belongings. He noticed a white envelope with his name written on it resting on the pillow. He tore into the envelope quickly to read this:

Dear Gabriel,

I'm sorry I'm not there to see you. I really wanted to be. I had so much fun with you and the guys a couple of weeks ago. While you're reading this, I'll be in the car driving with my father to our other camp, which is a little further west. He needed me to help him take care of a few things there. I'm hoping I can get back to see you soon. Ezra and Samuel will take good care of you. Until then, enjoy The River, and make sure you get to try Ezra's cinnamon rolls. They're amazing!

See you soon,

Tabitha

On one hand, Gabriel was thankful for the note, but on the other hand he was extremely disappointed. He had dreamt of seeing her, hugging her, and going for a long walk by the River. He was smitten by the way she smelled and by the way her hair felt on his cheek the last time they were together.

He set the note on his nightstand and joined Ezra on the deck. He sat down in the other rocking chair and put his feet up on the rail. After a few moments of silence, Ezra closed his book and leaned forward in his rocker with his elbows on his knees. Then he looked out at the water.

"Do you hear that?"

"Hear what?"

"Just listen. It's the sound of The River. It sounds different to me every night. It's like it's talkin' to ya. I don't know how it does that, but I'll tell you this, I never get tired of listenin.'"

"Hey, Ezra, what was that song you were singing when I met you earlier today?"

"I was singing? Oh, my . . . I don't know."

"You sounded great. Something about 'wade out in the water.'"

"Ah, yes." Ezra tipped his head back as he remembered. "My momma used to sing that when I was a little boy. I remember going down to The River and seeing some folks get baptized— you know, dunked under by a preacher. That was the song they sang at those gatherings. That's a real special memory for me."

The older man paused. "But that was a long time ago. Glad you're here, Gabriel Clarke." Then he got up and opened the door to his room.

He was almost inside when he leaned back out. "Tabitha said there is just somethin' about Gabriel. Ooh, she was smilin' when she said it, too."

Gabriel smiled back.

"Goodnight, Ezra."

CHAPTER 18

~ Hanging Out ~ With Ezra

A whole week had passed, and still no sign of Tabitha.

Gabriel was getting anxious to see her, but he hadn't summoned the courage to call the other camp to track her down. He didn't want to appear pushy.

With the arrival of summer warmth, the guide school was in full swing. The new guides were undergoing classroom training before and after receiving valuable hands-on clinics on The River. Like a summer football training camp, the Big Water coaches showed the incoming class what they needed to do to lead a raft down The River since one day they would actually make the calls in the whitewater.

Excitement filled the adventure camp as the first customers trickled in. The coming weekend—the opening of rafting season—promised to be a busy one.

Gabriel, who wasn't part of the guide school, busied himself with getting familiar with the workings of the camp. Ezra, who had him doing everything from cleaning the kitchen to patching rafts and washing wetsuits, showed him the ropes. Sure, he was doing grunt work, but anytime he wanted, he could enjoy the presence of The River and the majestic scenery.

His favorite part of the day was hanging out with Ezra on the deck overlooking the water after dinner. Ezra, blowing plumes of smoke from his pipe, dispensed anecdotes and bits of wisdom from his forty-plus years of working on The River. Many times, it seemed like Ezra knew him well because their conversations flowed as easily as the river waters passing by. Gabriel listened intensely and asked questions, but when there were lulls in the conversation, he turned to reading his trusted companion, The Journal.

At the end of the first week, Samuel approached Gabriel as he was finishing the last round of disinfecting the wetsuits and PFDs.

"I've got a three-raft group I'm taking tomorrow on a full-day Widowmaker run," Samuel announced. "There's a seat in my raft if you want to go. I'll need you to prep the lunches and be an overall assistant on the trip, though. If that sounds good to you, we hit it at nine o'clock sharp. Sound good?"

"Uh . . . yeah. Sounds good. I'm in." Gabriel played it cool, but he was excited. His adrenaline pumped as he remembered the exhilaration of running Widowmaker the first time with Tabitha. He immediately got that butterfly feeling in his stomach.

He was ready though.

He'd already conquered Widowmaker once and wanted more.

"I've never tasted stew that good before, Ezra. And that cornbread was like cake! I ate so much that I hurt myself. Where did you learn to cook like that?" Gabriel and Ezra were making their way back to the cabin after taking care of the kitchen clean-up.

"Aw, just doin' it, I suppose. When you make somethin' enough times, you figure out what went wrong and what went right. The important thing is you should never stop cookin'."

Gabriel felt like he was talking to an old friend. "All I know is there was a lot of love in that food. I'm no food connoisseur, but I can't imagine there being a better stew out there."

"Thank you, Gabriel. There's something very rewarding about cooking for folks. I love to see the looks on their faces when they take that first bite. Good food makes everything better. A good meal brings people together. What's better than that? Besides . . . I like to eat too." Ezra laughed heartily.

They made their way up to the deck attached to the back of their cabin. Within a few moments, though, a steady rain pelted the metal roof and picked up in intensity. Gabriel reached for The Journal and relaxed in his rocker. Ezra stood next to the deck railing, packing his pipe with fresh tobacco.

"So I hear you're going to run The River tomorrow with Samuel."

"Yeah, I'm looking forward to it. I'm a little nervous though."

"Nervous?" Ezra showed surprise in his voice.

"I've rafted The River only once. Don't forget—I grew up in Cairo, Kansas. We don't have falls like Widowmaker where I come from."

Ezra blew out a ring of lazy, pungent smoke. "You got it in ya blood, son. You'll have a great time. If this rain keeps up, it should make the water nice and fast tomorrow."

Gabriel didn't know how to respond.

Ezra broke the silence. "I love the rain. There's nothing more soothing than a rain at The River. The air gets thick, and I sleep like a baby."

Gabriel responded by changing the subject. "Do you know when Tabitha is coming?"

"Nope. With the way things are going, she may not be able to drop by any time soon. Apparently, they're short-handed at the other camp, so she may have to stay up there a while."

Gabriel's heart sank. He had visions of them spending time together on The River, like they did before.

"What? I've got to see her. I've been here a good week, Ezra."

The older man chuckled.

"What's so funny?"

"Nothin'. But tell you what. In a couple of days, we'll go see her. I think she'd like that. I hope you won't mind a two-and-a-half hour drive."

"Are you kidding? Not at all."

"We better clear it with Samuel first, so you ask him about

it tomorrow. We just need to get through the opening weekend, that's all."

Gabriel and Ezra took a break from talking and cracked open their books. For the last few nights, Gabriel had been slowly making his way through The Journal. He had read and reread several entries from his father and grandfather. He had found fascinating quotes, statements of honest frustration, and chronicles of harrowing close calls. Sentence by sentence, paragraph by paragraph, he was getting to know his family history. He was also getting to know The River.

As he was thumbing through the well-worn pages that evening, a page caught his eye. At the top, written in large bold letters, it said:

A Trusted Friend Who Can Cook

Gabriel read on.

November 14, 1953

Today was a better day, although I sense it may be soon. I'm weak and tired, and I don't like it at all, but that's the way it goes. My days have been good. I haven't always done the right thing, but I've tried. We all do the best we can and enjoy the journey.

The River has been good to me. I never tired of guiding people on The River. What a magnificent privilege it was to introduce people to the majesty. You don't have to say anything. Just take them there, and The River says it all. That'll be for John to carry on now. My son is a good man.

Today a good friend came to see me. He brought my favorite food, cinnamon rolls. It's not often you find someone in your life you can really trust, but Ezra Buchanan is one of those people. He's never asked for anything, and he always serves with a smile. I couldn't ask for a better co-worker or a better friend. I'm thankful The River brought us together.

I'll enjoy my treat now. I wonder if they'll have cinnamon rolls in heaven.

So long,

R. Allen Clarke

Gabriel felt like his heart stopped beating. A tidal wave of emotion washed over him. His grandfather, whom he never met, writing about his last days and the friend who was sitting in the rocking chair next to him. What a surreal moment.

"You knew my grandfather." Gabriel spoke with wonder in his voice.

"Yes, I did. Your father, too. I've been here a long time." Ezra kept on reading.

"So you knew who I was?" Gabriel knew he sounded a little indignant.

"Oh, yes. I was hoping you'd come back someday. Boy, you remind me of your father right now."

"How come you never said anything?"

"It's not for me to say when these things are talked about."

Ezra took his reading glasses off and looked at Gabriel. "I'm just glad you're here, son. This is where you belong."

The old man stood up. "Come with me. I have something to show you."

Ezra opened the sliding screen door to his room, and Gabriel followed him in. He could tell Ezra had lived there a long time. Inside the quaint room, there was a perfectly made bed, and a small tweed chair sat in the corner with a floor lamp next to it. Beside the lamp was a small wooden chest that he used as a footstool. Ezra knelt down and opened the top of the chest, and the smell of cedar wafted into the air.

"I made this chest many years ago. I keep some of my favorite little things in here."

Ezra pulled out a folder wrapped with a rubber band and dusted it off. He sat on the edge of his bed and opened the file, which contained a picture album full of black-and-white and sepia-tone pictures from the past.

"Look here. There's your dad when he was about twelve

standing with your grandfather. And there—those are the first customers at Big Water."

He flipped through a few more pages. "Ah, yes, there you are, Gabriel, with your daddy. Says here that you were three years old. Look at your face from all that crying. I remember that day well. You were so mad that you couldn't go rafting with him that day. Boy, you pitched quite a fit."

Gabriel stared in wonder at the picture of him and his father. His eyes welled, grateful for the ability to take in these scenes from his past.

"Could you tell me something about my father? About all I remember is playing marbles with him. I still have his marble collection. Most of my memories are so faint . . . overshadowed by one memory . . . the day I'd like to forget."

Ezra paused, lost in thought. "Your father was a great man, Gabriel. I could go on and on. He was strong as a bull. He'd do anything for anyone . . . give you the shirt off his back. He was very kind and patient. He knew The River. From the time he was a young boy, you could barely get him to come in and eat. He'd stay out by the water from dawn to dusk if he could. Yeah . . . I miss him, and your grandfather. They were very good to me."

Ezra put his hand on Gabriel's shoulder. "As for that one day you'd like to forget, I remember it well. You know how I like to think about it? I think of it as a special day . . . a day when something beautiful and something powerful happened—a man gave up his life to save another. It doesn't get any stronger than that in my book."

Gabriel sensed the respect and awe Ezra held for his father. He studied picture after picture and pondered what life had been like at the camp back then. After a few minutes, he came across a loose picture tucked in the back of the album. Black and white, with a corner torn, the picture showed Ezra standing next to his grandfather and his father when he was a young boy. They were all laughing, but Ezra was bent over looking at his father.

"Can you tell me about this picture?" Gabriel asked.

"Oh, yes, one of my favorite pictures. Your father was being quite ornery that day and getting into all kinds of mischief. He had a mad little look on his face because he didn't get his way or somethin'. Anyway, while we were getting ready to take that picture, your grandfather looked at your father and said, 'John, stand still for the picture. You better wipe that look off your face.' Your father replied by swiping the back of his hand across his mouth and then smiling from ear to ear."

Ezra demonstrated the gesture. "None of us could keep it together after that." They both shared a good laugh.

"One more question—how did you come to find my grandfather and work here at the camp?"

"He found me. I had no family and nowhere to go, but that's a whole other story."

Gabriel wanted to hear the story. "Can't you tell me?"

"Okay, but here's the real short version. One day, your grandfather saw me lying down next to the filling station in town. The weather had turned real cold, and I didn't know what I was going to do. All I had was the clothes on my back and a handful of marbles. Out of the blue, an angel named R. Allen Clarke asked me if I wanted a job. Forty-two years later, I'm still here. I'll be here as long as I'm welcome. Mister Clarke, he set my feet on solid ground."

The older man exhaled. "I'm getting kinda tired, so if it's fine with you I'm gonna turn in now."

Gabriel stood up to leave. "Hey, Ezra? You like to play marbles?"

Ezra's eyes beamed.

"I play a mean game of marbles, son."

———

The River had brought another wonderful surprise to Gabriel, and his name was Ezra Buchanan. Spending time with Ezra was like peering through a window into the epic landscape of whom he had come from. Every conversation with Ezra, like the stroke of a towel on a dirty windowpane, brought more and more clarity. Each conversation breathed new life into Gabriel.

For once, he was moving toward something.

And for the first time, he felt connected to the greatness of the legacy he came from . . . and who he was destined to become.

⌒ A WONDERFUL SURPRISE ⌒

June 27, 1952

I never tire of running The River.

I had two great runs today, and they both had magical things in store. First, I came across a couple of new strainers today near the Chutes. Then at the end of the day, I could tell that hydraulic at Widowmaker was getting deeper too. I had some great folks in my raft today.

One of my favorite things is introducing

first—timers to the beauty of The River. I'll never understand why some people choose not to connect. One man in my raft could focus only on what he left behind. He didn't seem to want to be here. He said he had too much to do, and he was here only because his wife wanted him to come.

Even though he was here, he missed it all— the beauty, the joy, the laughter, and the excitement. I hope he comes back to The River someday. Perhaps there is something about today's trip that will stay with him. Everything else pales in comparison. That man may go back to work and continue going up the ladder of success, or he may find that he leaned his ladder against the wrong building.

The River doesn't force itself on people; they have to choose to get in. That's what makes the waters so special. If you ask me, the pursuit of things can get in the way of what life is all about. I'm going to encourage every rafter to enjoy every moment and take nothing for granted.

I truly believe, once you experience The River, you find your way . . . I know I have.

John W. Clarke

In addition to reading some passages from The Journal before he fell asleep, Gabriel also started every morning studying the thoughts of his father and grandfather. If there was something he didn't understand or needed clarified, he'd ask other guides what the words meant. Sometimes he learned things about the art of running The River. Other times, the entries spoke to him about what it meant to be with The River.

Nearly every day, reading The Journal gave him a little more insight into his father's heart, as well as his grandfather's.

———◆———

A sensational aroma greeted Gabriel as he waltzed into the

kitchen around 8:30 a.m.

"Man, it smells like a bakery in here," Gabriel said, lifting his nose in the air.

"Wait until you try one, big guy. It'll change your life. I'm James."

The young man in his twenties with bushy black hair held out his hand.

"I'm Gabriel. Nice ukulele playing, by the way."

"Ah, thank you!"

"Here you go, gentlemen." Ezra, clad with large oven mitts and an apron that said "It's My Kitchen," held two iron skillets, one in each hand, full of fluffy, made-from-scratch cinnamon rolls. Sugary icing slathered on the top dripped down the side of the cinnamon rolls that everyone raved about. They all dug in, and the only sound was the moaning from the amazing taste and licking of sticky fingers.

"This is otherworldly, Ezra," James said.

"Amazing," was all Gabriel could muster.

"Thank you. I'm glad you're enjoying them." Several apprentice guides stopped in and polished off what was left.

"Five minutes, guys. Guests are arriving," Samuel bellowed from outside the kitchen screen door.

"Thanks, Ezra!" The rambunctious guides expressed their gratitude as they charged out the door.

"You boys have a safe day on The River," Ezra said.

It was opening weekend, and a dozen rafts were going out that day—an excellent warm-up for the season to come. On a good year, Big Water Adventure Camp hosted nearly ten thousand people at both camps.

The ground was soggy from heavy rains the night before. The sun could not be seen yet due to the height of the surrounding mountains, but light and warmth was spilling into the valley where The River flowed.

Ezra slid off his oven mitts and hung up his apron.

"Gabriel, let me take you down to the rigging shack. We'll get you started on prepping for trips."

"Sounds good," he replied.

The two made their way down a gravel drive toward a large barn-like structure that housed all the gear. Ezra unlatched a large door that creaked as he pulled it open.

Gabriel walked in and was taken aback by everything he saw. Countless rows of wetsuits hung eerily on the back wall. Wetsuit booties hanging by clothespins to drip dry lined the east wall. A huge rack of paddles were stacked in one corner, and several large crates—each labeled "Big," "Bigger," or "Biggest"—were overflowing with hundreds of helmets. The storage shed was cool and damp, and to Gabriel, all the rafting implements seemed to tell a story about The River. For some strange reason, the surroundings felt like home to him.

"Over there is where we keep the dry bags." Ezra pointed toward another corner of the storage shed. "That's what the clients use to keep their shoes and clothes from getting wet. The First Aid kits are in that cabinet over there. Oh, and all of the PFDs are on the other side of that wall," Ezra said during the quick walking tour.

"When you're with Samuel, he's very particular. He'll check

everything himself and then check it again. You pay close attention when you're with him, and you'll see how he does things. He's a good one to learn from."

No sooner than Ezra had finished his sentence when Samuel came in the back door with a stern look of concentration on his face.

"Speak of the devil," Ezra said.

Samuel walked over to the First Aid cabinet and snatched one off the shelves.

"Gabriel, I'm going to need you to grab a couple of the dry bags . . . "

Then the front door squeaked open. Gabriel turned to see who was there.

"Oh, my gosh!"

"Guess who!" Tabitha appeared looking as beautiful as ever, wearing her army green cargo pants and gray-hooded sweatshirt. She was a wonderful sight for Gabriel's eyes.

With Gabriel's heart pounding in excitement, the two embraced for several moments.

Ezra coughed into his hand. "I'm going to go check on the rafts. You kids have fun catching up." The older man moseyed back out the door.

"Hello, Miss Fielding," Samuel said, intent to stay on task.

"Hey, Samuel."

"Gabriel, grab two medium PFDs and meet me by the van in a few minutes."

With a First Aid bag in one hand, a dry bag in the other, and a wetsuit thrown over his shoulder, Samuel exited the storage shed.

"I wasn't sure when I'd get to see you." Gabriel's attention never left Tabitha. Their eyes locked together.

"I know. It seems like forever since that camping trip. Come out front. There's someone I want you to meet." Tabitha grabbed Gabriel's hand and led him out the front door, where he witnessed a loud greeting.

"Jacob, my man!"

Ezra was grasping hands in a brotherly handshake with a tall, gray-templed man wearing a faded blue baseball cap, sunglasses, and long-sleeved T-shirt that said *Live the River Life.*

"Ezra, please tell me you have a cinnamon roll left for me." His authoritative voice emanated from his six-foot, four-inch frame.

"Ha! I always keep one for you, Jacob."

Tabitha led Gabriel up to the man in his late forties.

"Dad, I want you to meet Gabriel Clarke."

Immediately, Gabriel felt the man's magnetism, as if he were meeting someone sure of who he was . . . sure of his calling.

"Gabriel, I'm Jacob Fielding. It's good to finally meet you." Jacob extended his hand to Gabriel and shook it firmly. He looked intensely right into Gabriel's eyes and squeezed even harder.

Gabriel met his strength. "Nice to meet you, sir."

Jacob took off his sunglasses. "So Tabitha tells me you're from Kansas."

"Yes, sir. For most of my life, anyway. Thank you for letting me come to work at the camp this summer."

"Thank *you*, Gabriel. When my daughter told me you might be coming, I was glad to hear that. After you're here for a while, I know you'll love The River as much as I do."

Gabriel responded to Jacob's confidence and enthusiasm. "The River is a special place. That's for sure."

"The River is more than a place, Gabriel. It's a way of living, really living. The River is alive and is constantly moving. Well . . . I look forward to spending some time with you while you're here. I just know you're going to love it . . . for many reasons." Jacob smiled as he looked over at his daughter.

Gabriel shuffled from one foot to another. "If it's anything like that trip I took a few weeks ago, I'm in."

"Yeah, I heard you guys had a blast. The River has a way of doing that to you, you know. A great man I knew used to say, 'Once you experience The River, you find your way.' Well, I've got a few things to take care of. I'll see you at dinner, young man." Jacob turned and headed back to the office.

Gabriel took note of his last statement. He was shocked to hear the words he read that morning in The Journal come out of Jacob's mouth. *Did he just say what I think he said?*

In their brief interaction, Gabriel felt drawn to Tabitha's father. He was so strong and confident, and even in their brief encounter, he emanated wisdom and a sense of acceptance.

Gabriel turned to Tabitha. "I better go meet Samuel. Are you rafting with us?"

"No. I need to stay here and help my dad with a few things. I'll catch up with you later. It's really good to see you, Gabriel."

They hugged one more time, and Gabriel went back to get his things and meet up with Samuel for their day trip.

It was about an hour before the rest of the rafters would arrive to sign forms and go through orientation. Gabriel joined Samuel and helped him load the back of the old van, which would tow the trailer stacked with rafts. Gabriel decided to break the silence.

"How long have you known Tabitha?" Gabriel asked.

"We've been friends a long time. Why?"

"Just curious. I think she's pretty amazing."

"She's a great girl. Good luck, though." A smirk crossed Samuel's face.

"What do you mean by that?"

"Just what I said. Maybe you'll have more luck than the rest of the guys who have tried to get to know her better."

Gabriel felt the awkwardness of the moment.

"Have there been a lot?"

"Are you kidding? A little fox like her? I think most every guide who has come through here thought she was *the one* at one time or another. Don't get your hopes up."

Gabriel sighed. "I think it's too late for that."

Their day on The River was fantastic. The trip filled the minds and hearts of each rafter with fantastic memories . . . and stories worth telling back at home. The weather turned out to be spectacular with sunny skies that painted the water with shafts of light. The water was high and fast because of the deluge the night before.

Gabriel kept a close eye on Samuel and learned everything he could from him. He watched how he served the rafters and gave them a wonderful experience. With every rapid traversed, every guide command heeded, every splash of cool water on his face, Gabriel's sense of connection with The River deepened.

After they returned to camp and bade the customers goodbye, Samuel opened up. "Man, that was a great run today, even though I thought that lady was going to freak out when she saw The Chutes."

Samuel's comment got Gabriel chuckling at the memory of the city dweller's jaw-dropping expression. "It's fun to see people conquer their fears, ya know?" Gabriel said.

"So how are you liking the whitewater world so far?" Samuel and Gabriel unloaded the trailer and hung the wetsuits to dry out behind the rigging shack.

"I'm loving every bit of it. This is going to be the best summer of my life. I just wish I would have realized sooner all the River had in store for me."

"Well, I'm glad you're loving it because you have good instincts out there. It's like you were meant for this stuff. When that guy from the other raft fell in and we came up beside him, the way you grabbed his vest and brought him in was perfect. He must have weighed two hundred-and-fifty pounds, and you made it look easy!"

"Must have been all those farm chores or something." Gabriel wore a sideways grin, trying not to show his excitement for the affirmation.

"Anyway, some of these guys come out here and don't take things seriously. I can tell you really respect things around here. Don't ever lose that sense of awe. You'll be guiding before you know it."

"I don't know about that. I don't think I know much of anything yet, and I think I'll be nervous running those rapids for a long time."

Samuel placed an arm on Gabriel's shoulder. "Listen, I've run The River hundreds of times, and right before I hit those rapids, I still get that butterfly feeling in my gut—and then that rush of adrenaline takes over. I think that feeling will always be there whenever you connect with something bigger than you. It's part of what makes life beautiful. If you stay connected only to that which is small enough for you to understand and control, then you have nothing—no adventure, no destiny, and no purpose."

Gabriel pondered what Samuel said. The depth of his words seeded deep into his mind and heart. The two finished stacking the paddles, dumping the helmets in their respective bins, and hanging up the booties and wetsuits to dry.

"Great job today," said the lead guide. "By the way, whenever Jacob comes for dinner at the beginning of the season, he pulls out all the stops. It usually involves the grill and red meat, two of my favorite things. You don't want to miss it."

"Believe me, I can't wait. See you there."

CHAPTER 20

A Dinner to Remember

A steady stream of black smoke ascended from the brick outdoor hearth just off the back of the main lodge. The tantalizing aroma of burning charcoal and the thought of eating barbecued meat from the grill got Gabriel's mouth watering. He couldn't think of a more perfect way to end a great day on The River.

Sunlight in the canyon had dimmed. The air was just cool enough, and the glow of gas lanterns on picnic tables and staked homemade torches illuminated the outdoor hangout. Shadows from the trees, like giant statues, emerged on the back wall of the lodge.

Gabriel peered at the iridescent full moon over the canyon wall. He was surrounded by whitewater protégés milling in small groups, catching up on the activities of the day. Like improvisational music, the sounds of conversation and laughter echoed around the camp—another sign of a great season to come on The River.

Gabriel found Jacob and Ezra standing in front of the six-foot-wide barbecue, poking the coals and adding a few hickory sticks for flavor.

"I think we're ready to grill," Jacob announced. "Bring on the meat, boys!" His declaration earned a few whoops.

"Gabriel, could you help me?"

Gabriel looked up and saw Tabitha standing at the porch door leading to the kitchen.

"Glad to," he replied, and he followed her into the kitchen, where he saw two large tin trays piled high with rib eye steaks.

"Look at all this meat! There's enough here to feed a small army."

Tabitha lifted one of the trays and gave it to Gabriel. "My dad doesn't do anything small. When he throws a party, it's all out."

"I guess so." Gabriel shook his head as they each carried a tin tray out to Ezra and Jacob. As they made their way through the picnic tables, several guys clapped. Feeling conspicuous, Gabriel glanced at Tabitha with a puzzled look on his face.

"I guess they're pretty excited about this dinner, huh?"

"Dad likes a festive atmosphere. He loves to celebrate."

The smell of the flame-kissed rib eye steaks cooking over the open fire was pure heaven. Ezra, wearing his trademark red apron, kept flipping the juicy steaks so they wouldn't burn to a crisp.

With a nod of the head from Ezra, Jacob cupped his

hands over his mouth and called out, "Rib eyes are ready! Let's dig in!"

Everyone moved in quickly to receive his or her piece of char-grilled goodness. Hot baked potatoes wrapped in tin foil as well as generous hunks of Ezra's famous cornbread filled their plates. Once everyone had been served, Ezra took off his apron and passed through the chow line. He joined Jacob, Tabitha, and Gabriel at the table closest to The River.

Gabriel carved off a tip of the expertly grilled rib eye and took his first bite. He swooned in delight, and then grinned in Ezra's direction. "This steak is amazing. What did you season it with?"

"Just a little salt and pepper and a few other goodies. I can't tell you all my secrets the first week you're here."

"Man, it's incredible."

"Glad you like it," Jacob said. "I believe in bringing out the best to celebrate new friends . . . and old ones." Jacob smiled at Ezra, who tipped his hat in recognition. Then Jacob stood up to get everyone's attention, prompting Ezra to tap his water glass with his knife.

When the boisterous group had calmed down, Jacob began. "Hey, everyone. I'd like to say once again how excited I am about a new season. I'm thankful for each one of you coming to help us out this summer. How's your food?"

Everyone responded with a hearty cheer, and even a few whistles erupted.

"I just want to say I believe this will be our best year yet. Between Big Water and the North Camp, we're going to introduce thousands of people to The River. What a gift and a privilege. Whether you're guiding a raft, working the front desk, helping out Ezra in the kitchen, or even cleaning the bathrooms, you are vital to serving those who come to experience everything The River has to offer. Each one of you fulfills a different role, but we are all equally important."

Jacob shifted his weight before continuing. "I don't believe in accidents. You are here for a reason. Don't ever think that you're not vitally important to the mission. Remember, there's only one *you*, so bring your best. No one can do that for you."

Gabriel was mesmerized by what Jacob had to say. He had never heard anyone talk like this. Each sentence resonated with him.

"Your dad really has a way with words," Gabriel said to Tabitha.

"Oh, he's always been like that." She paused, then rested her hand on Gabriel's forearm. "That means a lot to me . . . that you notice."

Gabriel's heart skipped a beat. Tabitha shared that special gift of knowing what to say at just the right time.

Jacob raised his right hand into the air. "There's one other thing I want to say, and it's about how excited I am that Gabriel Clarke has come to The River this year. So Gabriel, it's great to welcome you into the fold. May your time on The River be something you will never forget."

Jacob paused for a second, almost as if he needed to collect himself. "Let's raise one to good friends . . . to good food . . . and to The River!" Everyone toasted their soda bottles and iced tea glasses, and a chorus of laughter and frivolity ensued.

The sense of celebration was intoxicating. The joy in the camp took Gabriel to a new place—a place where he could allow himself to be happy. He realized that he was discovering a newfound freedom—the freedom to enjoy being alive.

He didn't know everyone that well yet, but they shared something in common. They had all been captured by the beauty of The River and felt compelled to share it with others who came their way. Even though they had come from different parts of the country, even the world, he had felt accepted. These people wanted *him* there.

He was becoming one of them.

There was hardly a moment of silence during dinner. The stories circulating around the tables brought raucous rounds of laughter, and animated conversation filled the camp for a couple of hours. Gabriel, Tabitha, Ezra, and Jacob's table was no different. Jacob regaled them with hilarious "city slicker" stories about the colorful characters who drove high into the mountains to experience the great outdoors, only to exit their Cadillacs in garish Bermuda shorts and black wingtips. Ezra recounted the pranks the guides would play on one another, like the time when one guide forged a "Dear John" letter to a lovesick roommate. Ezra's stories seemed funnier because the older man had a formal and dignified way about him.

Shortly after nine o'clock, Ezra stood up. "If you will excuse

me, everyone. I believe it's time for me to retire for the evening." As the longtime chef made his way around the eating area, he collected dishes and stacked them on his arms. When Tabitha joined him, Jacob turned his focus to Gabriel.

"I've noticed that you haven't said too much tonight. I apologize if we monopolized the conversation."

"Are you kidding?" Gabriel exclaimed. "I love hearing these stories. This has been amazing."

"We've lived a lot of life at The River, that's for sure. Everyone has a story though. Tell me about Kansas. What's life like there?"

"There's not really that much to tell." Gabriel looked down and picked at the splinters of wood in the picnic table.

"I bet there's a lot to tell. I'm listening."

Gabriel sighed for a moment. "I'm from a little town called Cairo. It's really small. I've lived there with my mom since I was four years old. We live in a rented room off the back of the Cartwrights' farmhouse. The Cartwrights have been like grandparents to me, I guess. My mom works really hard at the Cairo Diner. It hasn't been easy, but we've managed. I'll tell you this: Kansas doesn't look anything like Colorado."

"So what's good about living in Cairo?" Jacob continued his incisive questions.

"I don't know. Miss Vonda makes amazing fried chicken, and Mister Earl introduced me to fishing . . . I love to fish."

"Ah, food and fishing—two of my favorites as well."

Gabriel felt comfortable with Jacob, so he mentioned something that he'd never told anybody. "I've known some good people back home and had some good times, but I've always sensed I don't belong there—I don't know—like I wasn't made for Kansas."

"Really?"

Gabriel noticed that Jacob was looking him directly in the eye.

"Well, I just want to remind you that I'm really glad you're here, and I'm looking forward to getting to know you better."

Jacob switched gears. "I have an idea. Do you have any plans for the rest of evening?"

"Not at all. I was just going to read some before turning in."

Jacob looked up into the sky. "The moon is really bright tonight . . . why don't you meet me over at my Jeep in about fifteen minutes."

"Great. Where are we going?"

"You'll see. Fifteen minutes." Jacob smiled as he took the last swig of his drink and got up from the picnic bench.

Gabriel was excited, intrigued, and a bit nervous by the sudden invitation. He had heard Jacob was a spontaneous man.

At the same time, though, after only one dinner together, he felt like he had known Jacob his entire life.

———————

Gabriel walked up to the faded red 1959 Jeep CJ-5. Jacob pulled some rope out of the back and threw it on the ground. Then he pulled off his long-sleeved buttoned shirt and reached for a white T-shirt lying in his Jeep.

Gabriel couldn't help but notice a one-inch wide nasty scar that ran from the top of Jacob's shoulder down the back of his arm to his elbow. He didn't want to say anything about the disfigurement to Jacob, but he was curious about what happened.

Jacob finished putting the T-shirt on.

"Come with me," he commanded.

Gabriel followed him over to the back of the rigging shack.

"Here, grab the other side of this," he said. Jacob walked over to a heap of fully inflated rafts stacked on top of another.

This really got Gabriel thinking. Jacob motioned for him to grab a side of the raft on top of the stack, and together they carried it over to the Jeep, where they hoisted the raft onto the cross bars. Jacob then collected the rope from the ground to anchor the raft to the rack.

"Go grab yourself a PFD, a paddle, and a dry bag. I've got mine in the Jeep."

Gabriel did as he asked. Jacob fired up the engine, and they rolled out of the camp.

"Are we actually going on The River . . . at night?"

"Yup. You're going to love this. It's a beautiful night to be on The River."

Though he felt safe with Jacob, Gabriel could feel the butterflies fluttering in his gut. He pushed those feelings aside, though, as they weaved through the canyon on the bumpy mountain road. The cliffs rose sharply on the right side of the

Jeep, and the dim headlights barely lit the path ahead. With every shift of the manual transmission, the old jeep jerked and chugged in the darkness.

"You ever been on The River at night?"

"Are you kidding? It was all I could do to get on The River in broad daylight." Gabriel shocked himself a little at his own transparency.

"Well, there's something about The River at night, when it's just you, the water, and the light of the moon."

"How do you navigate though? I mean . . . the rocks and waterfalls. Isn't that kind of dangerous?"

"It can be."

Then why are we doing this? Is this guy crazy? Gabriel rolled all kinds of thoughts around in his head.

"You see, Gabriel, there are things about The River that you can experience only when it's dark. The River reveals itself differently at night. It's difficult to explain. I listen and watch more closely when I don't know exactly what's next. My connection to The River is deeper in the night."

"I think I know what you mean." Gabriel recalled his middle-of-the-night experience at The River from just a couple of weeks earlier.

"Of course, you want to ride The River at night only when you know the waters really well. I've been here my whole life. I know The River. I mean, you can't know *everything* about it, but I know The River well enough. I've studied it. I've spent time on it. Not a day goes by that I don't connect with The River."

Jacob paused for a moment. "I've made a lot of mistakes

here at The River, Gabriel . . . but I've learned from them."

The older man quickly changed the subject. "Hey . . . look at this!" Jacob pointed to the left side of the road and slowed down to a stop. A small black bear was foraging through greenery. When he heard the Jeep slow, the cuddly creature looked back over his shoulder in their direction, his eyes reflecting a bright green shine.

"Oh, wow! Look how cute the little fella is!" Gabriel exclaimed with hushed excitement.

"Yeah, they're cute, but their mommas are never too far away. Momma bears will do anything to protect their babies. I learned that one the hard way. I tried to get up close to a cub one time, and then I heard a nasty growl that I still can't get out of my head. I kept backing up until she had me cornered against The River."

"What did you do?"

"I had only one option. I jumped into The River and rode it. That was a pretty bumpy swim . . . I don't recommend it."

Jacob put the Jeep in gear and rumbled up the road again. He drove about a half mile more and turned off into a clearing.

"Okay . . . let's do it!" Jacob jumped out of the Jeep, and Gabriel followed. The two untied the raft and lugged it down about thirty yards to The River's edge. They gathered their paddles, PFDs, and dry bags and secured them in the raft.

"So, how are we going to get back to the Jeep?" Gabriel asked.

"Tabitha will drive here with one of the other guides to pick up my truck. Then she'll drop it off down river for us.

Otherwise, that would be a really long walk back. Oh, yeah. It's important to have one of these."

Jacob held up a large metal flashlight. He smiled as he flicked it on and off a couple of times, which made Gabriel feel a little better. "It doesn't matter how well you know The River, it's still important to keep a light with you. You never know what will try to spoil your experience."

"I was hoping you'd have something like that." Gabriel flashed a grin.

The two donned their PFDs and cinched them tightly. They slid the yellow raft into the water and climbed in.

The water was silky smooth and beautiful. The moon shone brightly and covered the water's surface with a soft glow. With one stroke of Jacob's paddle, the vessel glided into the middle of The River.

The air was still and crisp and the canyon silent. Like a cosmic glitter sprinkled across the midnight sky, the infinite number of stars twinkled with radiant brilliance.

The next few hours held exciting new discoveries for Gabriel. Little by little, the frightened, lost boy from Kansas was coming out of his protective shell.

This night with Jacob . . . and The River . . . would change everything.

CHAPTER 21

THE NIGHT RUN

The slight gulping sound from a pair of paddles dipping into the water ever so gently was all that could be heard in the canyon.

Perched on opposite sides of the raft—Gabriel in front and Jacob in back—the two men floated for the first hour, taking in the smell of the spruce and fir trees while marveling at the starlit canopy above. Gabriel felt such a sense of freedom and connection during this evening run on The River—even more than in daytime. The feeling was mysterious, hauntingly eerie, and beautiful all at the same time. Knowing it was just the two of them—intertwined with the wilderness and The River—gave Gabriel the feeling that he was experiencing something special, unique, and powerful. He reached his arm down the side of the raft and just as his fingers touched the water, two loud howls echoed through the canyon and startled him.

"Whoa! What was that?" Gabriel looked back at Jacob.

"Shhh . . . listen." Jacob put his finger up to his mouth.

After a few moments of silence, the howls began again. This time there were more baying, one after the other. Each howl had a little different tone and pitch. The wolf-like cries seemed to develop a sense of asymmetrical rhythm and continued for several minutes.

"It's like they are singing or something," Gabriel commented with amazement. "Why do they do that?"

Jacob lifted his paddle out of the water. "Oh, for lots of reasons. When wolves venture out and search for food, keeping the pack together is paramount. What we could be hearing is a reunion call—a call to stay together, to notify the others if they've found food, or to send a message to potential enemies that the pack will protect its own. Some speculate their 'singing' strengthens their relationship to each other. Humans could learn a lot from wolves."

As the howling chorus became more distant, the sound of whitewater escalated. Gabriel gripped his paddle harder as the current picked up. The moonlight remained strong as they made a slow bending turn. The glow of splashing whitewater could be seen down the canyon corridor.

Jacob continued musing about his experience. "That's what's so incredible about being on The River at night. Even in a full moon you really can't see exactly how The River is moving . . . so you have to listen. When you listen intensely in the dark, you hear and experience things you would never notice in broad daylight."

"I've been noticing that."

"Good. Now are you ready?"

"Ready as I'll ever be!" Gabriel took a few deep breaths and tried to pump himself up as he prepared to run the whitewater by the light of full moon.

"Just listen close to my commands. We aren't going to run anything over a Class II or III tonight so don't worry. I wouldn't put you in danger. Okay?"

Gabriel turned around and responded to Jacob's reassurance.

"Okay."

The pace of the water livened, and the sound of rapids caused Gabriel's pulse to quicken. Vision was limited, which made the pace seem even faster. Gabriel could feel the water slapping his feet under the raft.

"Forward hard, Gabriel! Stay in the middle!"

Gabriel dug his paddle in deep and pulled. The first large rapid arrived. The nose of the raft dove down and collided with a small wave, spraying water into Gabriel's face. The fact that they had such dim light made the waves seem like they had twice the size and strength.

"Yeah! There we go! Beautiful!" Jacob's celebratory exclamations brought even more courage to Gabriel. "Isn't that great?"

"Woo-hoo! Yeah!" Gabriel joined in, exhilarated to be on nature's roller coaster.

The raft bobbed up and down on the swift and strong water. Like a skier navigating moguls, they plunged over and around the waves, splashing and careening through the canyon. For several minutes, the action was non-stop: fast, strong, and rough. Jacob then informed Gabriel that they were coming to the end of this series of rapids but there would be a big one at the finish.

"Get ready, Gabriel! When I say 'now,' lean in and hold on!"

The noise got louder as the thunderous water splashed over the rocks. Gabriel's heart raced with joy. The thrill was like nothing else. It was just he and Jacob, drinking in The River on a spectacular night.

"Now!" Jacob shouted.

Gabriel lunged into the center of the raft and braced himself, grabbing onto a canvas handle. The River dropped out from under the raft and swooped down, crashing into a thick wave at the bottom. That prompted a wall of water to cascade over Gabriel's head as the raft lunged forward and past the torrent.

"Yeah! Yeah! Yeah!" Gabriel roared a victory cry as he wiped water out of his eyes. "Amazing!"

"I told you, buddy! I knew you'd love it." Jacob was smiling from ear to ear at the ignition of Gabriel's passion.

They spent the next hour and half running light rapids, enjoying the midnight solitude, bantering back and forth and getting to know each other. The bond between the two deepened with every stroke of the paddle.

"Let's head over to that clearing over there. This is one of my favorite places to stop and enjoy The River." Jacob used his paddle as a rudder to guide their raft through the easy flow and up onto the beach.

"Recognize anything?"

Jacob handed the young man a large flashlight out of his dry bag. Gabriel stepped out and pulled the raft up on the clay-colored dirt. He switched on the light, aiming the beam around the cove. He noticed an abandoned fire pit, then looked over his shoulder quickly and saw a fallen log near the water. Then he shot the flashlight beam onto the water, which illuminated a large rock in the middle of The River.

"Hey! I know this place. That rock was where I found one of my marbles."

"A marble?"

"It's a long story. I'll tell you later."

"Do that. Hey, isn't this a great spot? I love coming to 'The Beach,' as we call it. It's a great place to slow down and take it in, being on The River. I don't do that as often as I should." Jacob took a deep breath and sighed.

A solitary fluffy cloud slowly drifted east, revealing more moonlight and brightening the cove. Jacob pulled a couple of towels out of his dry bag and handed one to Gabriel.

"It gets a little chilly at night when you're wet."

"To be honest, I hadn't really noticed. This is all just surreal." Gabriel sat down on the log, wiping his face and neck with the towel. Jacob sat down a few feet away.

"What do you mean?"

"What I'm experiencing here is so much different from my life in Kansas. It's like I'm part of some dream or something.

A few days ago, my boss griped about the way I stacked boxes at the Five & Dime, and now I'm out here on The River. The difference is hard to put into words. It's like a whole other world."

"I'm glad you like it here."

"What's not to like? Everything about The River is breathtaking."

They both stared out at the softly lit water. "No question about that. It is beautiful here." Jacob paused. Then his tone became more serious. "I know why you like it so much here, Gabriel."

"Really?"

"Yeah. I believe it's more than just the beauty of The River. You were meant to be here from the beginning. Kansas was never your true home. You were born here. You're family roots are here. You were made for The River, Gabriel."

The silence was deafening. Gabriel was moved deeply by Jacob's words. He spoke deliberately with such kindness and authority.

Jacob continued with his thoughts. "I think you like The River so much because *this* is your home. I knew of your family when you were just a little boy. Your grandfather was a legend around here . . . your father, too. They knew The River better than anyone. Their camp at Corley Falls was one of the first of its kind. I'll never forget hearing about their exploits. They were known not only for their knowledge of The River, but their love for it. John Clarke was a great man, Gabriel. I see his greatness . . . I see him in *you*."

Gabriel could hardly breathe. Between the kindness and love he felt from Jacob and the grief he still carried, the torrent of emotion welled up in him like a geyser. His eyes pooled with tears as he bowed his head and looked at the ground. Sniffling and through his quivering lips, he managed to reply.

"My memories of him are few . . . but they are so vivid. He was really strong, and he played with me whenever he could. I loved it when he threw me up in the air. I never worried about hitting the ground. He always caught me. I didn't have much time with him, but I miss him so much."

Jacob, who appeared to be choking back tears, put his hand on Gabriel's shoulder.

"I'm so sorry. I just want you to know that I'm here if you need anything . . . anything at all. I mean that. Whatever you need . . . okay?"

Jacob patted him couple of times, then wiped his eyes. Their poignant conversation was joined by a loud screech that echoed in the canyon.

Gabriel picked up the flashlight and rose to his feet.

"I know that sound." He shined the narrow beam across the water and onto the opposite canyon wall.

"Where are you?" he said toward the noise.

The screech happened again. This time, Gabriel shone the light slowly onto the trees jutting out of the rocky wall.

"There you are!"

Like a guardian of the canyon, an albino red-tailed hawk rested on a tree branch in clear view just a hundred yards away.

"Do you see her, Jacob? She was around when we camped here a few weeks ago. She followed me all day on that river trip. It's like she knows I'm here or something."

"That's one beautiful hawk. Quite rare, too. I don't think I've ever heard one call like that at night."

Jacob slapped his hands. "What do you say we finish our trip? We don't have too much further to go before we get to the Jeep."

"Isn't there some pretty aggressive water ahead?" Gabriel hadn't forgotten what happened on his first trip.

"You must be talking about Widowmaker. Yeah, that's a fun but crazy stretch of water. But we won't be running those falls at night. We'll take out before we get there."

Gabriel exhaled in relief. "Hey, can I show you something before we go?"

"Of course."

Gabriel reached into his dry bag and pulled out a twice-folded piece of paper. He opened the sheet and held it in his left hand while shining the flashlight with his right.

"I have a journal from my father and grandfather that my mom gave me. It has all kinds of writings about their time with The River. This morning, I copied a portion from one of my father's entries, and I've been thinking about it a lot. With everything you said . . . well . . . I thought you'd like to read it."

Gabriel scooted closer to Jacob, who fixed his eyes on the crinkled, handwritten note. He read aloud the following entry:

For my son—

Gabriel, I hope you experience The River someday as I have. To see you become a river guide would be a dream come true for me. Only you can make that decision for yourself someday. Great adventure awaits you. Don't ever settle for the shore, Gabriel. Get all the way in.

I see courage in you. Even as a three-year-old, you seem ready to take on the world. I long for the day when we can run The River together. You are my little champion. I hope when you are able to read this someday, you will realize that you were made for The River.

Dad

Jacob kept staring at the note for a long time.

"I have no words, Gabriel. That is truly remarkable. And to think your father thought to write these things down . . . amazing."

"I've been reading The Journal nonstop since Mom gave it to me. I can't tell you how incredible it's been to hear from my father all these years later. Through his writings, he's teaching me the ways of The River. The best thing of all is that I'm getting to know how much he really loved me."

Gabriel folded up the paper and put it back in his bag. "Thanks again for bringing me out here."

"Thank *you*, my friend."

It was well past midnight now, dipping into the morning hours.

For Gabriel, time had flown by on The River. The two men gathered their things and embarked on the last few minutes of their trip together. The last half-mile of water was gentle and peaceful, allowing them to reflect on their journey.

This evening of adventure and camaraderie moved Gabriel closer to his destiny . . . closer to The River. He felt like he and Jacob formed a seemingly unbreakable bond that night.

It was a bond that would be tested to its limits.

CHAPTER 22

The War Room

A few days had passed since Gabriel ran The River with Jacob that night. Big Water Adventure camp was in full swing. Guests were coming in greater numbers every day, and Gabriel loved this new season of his life.

There was really no part of life on The River that he wasn't thankful for. From morning until night, he gleaned all he could from the experience. He loved being around Jacob, learning from this icon of river rafting, who by his presence alone infused life and confidence in him. In addition, his evening conversations with Ezra on the deck were always a welcome end to the busyness of the days, but nothing topped the time he spent with Tabitha. Their times together were never enough.

Since she was just visiting from North Camp, they usually worked on different tasks throughout the day, so meal times were definitely a highlight for Gabriel. They always sat together, and if they were talking about something interesting, they flirted with each other incessantly. This clear mountain morning started no differently than others with a breakfast of iron-skillet cooked eggs, sausage, biscuits, and coffee.

Gabriel finished chewing and swallowed his bite of biscuit and jam. "This food is so good. It's hard to stop eating! Good thing your dad has me working so much. Otherwise, I'd be a blimp."

Tabitha chuckled. "I don't think you have to worry about that. Come here." She motioned with her hand to Gabriel and then pointed to her chin.

"You have a little something right here." She reached over and wiped a biscuit crumb from Gabriel's getting-scruffier-by-the-day beard.

"Thanks." The two locked eyes as she blotted the speck from his face.

"My dad and I have to head back up to the North Camp today to take care of some things. Dad is teaching a guide class right now, and I have a little time before we leave. You wanna take a walk with me?"

"Absolutely, Miss Fielding."

They cleared their dishes and headed out of the dining area to a well-worn path that circled the camp running right along The River's edge. Tabitha reached out and took hold of Gabriel's hand and snuggled close to his side. Her head pressed into his shoulder as they walked.

"I wish I could stay here with you."

"Me too," Gabriel replied gently.

"So there isn't anyone back in Kansas? Any . . . girl?"

"What? No, no . . . no girl back there for me." Gabriel chuckled nervously. "The only girl who really spoke to me in high school was Selma Eldridge. Selma was nice, but she never looked me in the eye when she talked—and oh, could she talk. I'm pretty sure she didn't need to breathe when she was telling a story. Funny thing about her. She always smelled like peanut butter. I like peanut butter and all, but that just didn't work for me."

Tabitha burst into laughter and playfully slapped him on the arm.

"That's not nice. Poor Selma. She just thought you were handsome."

"I know . . . I'm sorry."

The couple stopped walking, and Tabitha moved in front and faced Gabriel. The water babbled over the smooth stones in the shallow current of The River as the trees swayed with an intermittent breeze. Tabitha looked straight up into Gabriel's eyes.

"Well . . . there may not have been a girl in Kansas for you . . . but there's one in Colorado."

Tabitha stood on her tiptoes and closed her eyes. Gabriel leaned down and met her with a tender kiss. For Gabriel, the world stopped in that moment. Her hands holding tightly to his shoulders, his hands resting around her waist, this seemed to make it official for Gabriel. He was in love and completely captured by this young fox. The two continued kissing for several seconds before she broke the connection.

"Is everything okay?" Gabriel was nervous he did something wrong.

"Yeah . . . yeah, everything is really great." Tabitha smiled. "I just have to go soon . . . and I don't want to." She gave him a peck on the cheek. "Let's go over here."

Simmering in the glow of their encounter, the two sauntered along the path that took them away from The River and back into the woods. They heard the sound of a solitary voice talking in the distance.

"That's Dad. He's getting revved up teaching the greenhorns."

Just a few paces ahead, they came upon a large one-room, shed-like structure, up on stilts to compensate for the uneven ground at the base of the hill. The rugged building could fit about forty people in a classroom setting. With large plywood flaps for window coverings that could be raised and lowered by a rope and pulley, the rustic structure was a mountain cabana of sorts. At the front of the room was a large chalkboard and small handmade podium. Tabitha lowered her voice as the two approached the small building from the east side.

"Dad calls this 'The War Room,' " she whispered. "It's where he does his safety talks and planning sessions."

"The War Room?"

"Yeah. He lectures rookies and hammers out 'battle' strategies, as he calls them. He wants every guide to be as prepared as possible for anything that could happen on The River. I'm telling you that he's serious about safety."

They moved in and sat down on the ground and leaned

against the shed. They were perched underneath a wide-open back window so they couldn't be seen. Jacob's voice became crystal clear as Gabriel and Tabitha tuned in.

"There is nothing more amazing than running The River. That's why you're here. The River has captured you too. When you experience the majesty and grandeur of The River, it's breathtaking. What a privilege it is to enjoy such beauty . . . to experience such power. So respect it. Stand in awe of it. The River is infinitely bigger than any of us and deserves our very best. I want to challenge you to not just be around The River but to really study it. Get to know The River. The more you get to know, the more your knowledge will ignite your passion, and that will spill over every day as you guide others. This is bigger than a job, guys—it's a way of life! Some of you will join us here, and sure, you'll learn all the technical stuff, but you'll never really immerse yourself fully in what the water has to offer you. It's about the journey, man! The River will teach you new and exciting things every day."

A momentary pause broke Jacob's enthusiasm, and the pace and volume of his monologue dropped. "I took so much of this for granted when I was young. I did some childish things . . . stupid things. While there is so much joy and adventure in running The River, if you don't pay attention . . . if you don't work together . . . if you don't really prepare yourself and understand what's in play, bad things can happen. Life and death are in the balance, and when you don't respect that, you could die, plain and simple. Or worse yet, someone else could die."

Gabriel didn't move a muscle as he listened to Jacob's

passionate speech. He stood up just tall enough to peer over the back windowsill. Standing in the shadows, he was just out of Jacob's line of sight. Tabitha stood on her tiptoes to sneak a peek as well.

A dozen students scattered around the stark room sat in old wooden chairs. They were focused, hanging on every word without a peep. Jacob scooted his podium to the side and moved closer to the apprentices. He unbuttoned his plaid oxford shirt and took it off, leaving his fit torso in just a gray undershirt. Jacob draped the outer shirt on the podium and turned with his right shoulder to the students. With his left hand, he pulled his right sleeve up over his shoulder, revealing a horrific scar that Gabriel had noticed before.

"You see that? That's Mercy. I name my scars, by the way."

Jacob flashed a quick grin. No one knew whether to laugh or not because that was one nasty scar.

He continued in a grateful tone. "Mercy reminds me every day what could have happened to me. But I have to tell you something: this scar doesn't hurt anymore. It's a visible reminder, though, of a rock that took a bite out of me when I kayaked over some falls that I had *no business* navigating. Mercy reminds me I deserved to die that day, but for some reason I didn't. This scar is a reminder to be thankful for everything . . . thankful for life. Mercy also reminds me of greatness . . . but not my greatness."

Tabitha's father looked down at the scar again, his eyes moist and red. "Mercy reminds me of the greatness of The River . . . and the greatness of the man who lost his life saving mine."

A bone-chilling silence fell over the room. No one moved as Jacob put his shirt back on.

Gabriel listened intently as Jacob carried on with the story.

"My decisions cost a man his life, and I will have to live with that until the day I die. A family lost a son that day. A little boy . . . lost a father. To tell you the truth, I've wanted to give up many times. I was in a dark place for many years. But I was given a second chance, so rather than give up and be swallowed by my guilt, I chose to do what I believe he would have wanted me to do—dedicate my life to The River and to those who come my way to experience it. That's what my life has been about for the last sixteen years, and that's what it will always be about. I want to honor John Clarke's legacy in every way possible."

When Gabriel heard his father's name, time froze. Everything went silent. Jacob kept speaking, but each word blurred into the other. It was all white noise to him. With glazed eyes, hands on his head, he turned, leaned his back up against the building, and slid down to the ground slowly, ending up in a heap of disbelief and confusion. Mortified by the implications of what he just heard, he could hardly process the stunning revelation.

"Gabriel. Gabriel. Are you okay? What's wrong?" Tabitha grabbed his arm to get his attention, but Gabriel was lost in his own world.

Memories of that day flooded Gabriel's mind in an instant. The lifeless man in the kayak . . . his father's words . . . "I'll be

right back, Gabriel!" . . . the thunder of the waterfall . . . and his daddy disappearing beneath the blue-green torrent. Those Kodachrome images kept appearing in his mind's eye. If that man . . . if Jacob . . . had not been so irresponsible, they would have finished their marble game that day . . . and that little boy would have grown up with his father.

I can't believe this is happening.

My father died that day, saving Jacob's life.

And Tabitha's father was to blame?

"I have to go." Gabriel stood up, shrugging Tabitha's hand away.

"Gabriel! What is it?"

No response.

Walking slowly back down the path and numbed by the news, Gabriel returned to The River's edge. He took a seat on a large moss-covered rock that jutted out into the gentle waters. After a few minutes of solitude, he heard footsteps but didn't turn his gaze from The River. Tabitha joined him out on the boulder.

"I thought I'd find you here. Please tell me what's wrong," Tabitha pleaded.

"I think you know. Why didn't he tell me?"

Gabriel turned to Tabitha and lashed out in a more aggressive tone. "Why didn't *you* tell me?"

"Dad wanted to. He was just waiting for the right time. All these years he had wondered about you."

"Everything he said, about wanting to be there for me . . . is that what all this is about? Is he just trying to make himself feel better for what *he* did? I can't believe this."

"It's not like that. You have to believe me."

Tabitha leaned in to hug him, but Gabriel turned a cold shoulder.

"Well, what *is* it like then? It seems like a man that I was really beginning to admire is the man who made really bad choices, and those choices ended up costing my father his life . . . his life, Tabitha!"

Tabitha responded through her tears. "He's sorry. He's so sorry. You heard him. He wants to honor your father. He wants to honor you. No one can bring your father back, but we can honor his legacy by how we move on."

"Please don't tell me to move on."

"That's not what I meant to—"

Gabriel interrupted her. "I can't do this right now, Tabitha. I'm sorry."

Confused, angry, and shattered, Gabriel left Tabitha on the rock and retreated to his room.

———◆◆◆———

After Jacob's class was over, Tabitha saw her father heading back toward the front office. She ran down the path and intercepted him just before he got there. A little out of breath and frantic, she stopped him in his tracks.

"Dad, Gabriel and I were out walking, and we ended up sitting outside the War Room. Gabriel heard you talk about the scar and John Clarke."

The tears began to flow, her palm rubbing her forehead. "He's really upset, Dad. I don't know what to do."

"Where is he?"

"I don't know. His room maybe."

———————◆◆◆———————

Jacob didn't say anything more. He headed straight back down the path, through the woods to Ezra and Gabriel's cabin. He walked up the steps onto the deck and knocked on Gabriel's door.

"Gabriel?"

He waited.

"Gabriel?" This time, he said his name a little louder.

Gabriel opened the door slowly about halfway.

"Yeah?"

"I guess we need to talk."

"I don't have anything to say, Jacob."

"Would you come sit down with me for a second?"

Gabriel quietly came out on the deck and leaned up against the rail. His face was stern and his body language cold.

"I can only imagine how difficult this is for you, and I mean that. I can only imagine. Please just hear me out, Gabriel."

Gabriel's silence seemed to give him permission.

"I had been waiting for the right time to talk to you about all this, but quite frankly, I was scared. You see, I've wondered about you all these years. I can't tell you how deeply sorry I am for everything that happened. There's not a day that goes by that I don't think about what happened that day . . . or that I don't think about you. I have been haunted by my actions for years. I would do anything to take it all back if I could."

Jacob's lip quivered. "I just hope you can forgive me, Gabriel. Please forgive me." He sniffled and wiped both eyes.

Gabriel did not muster a reply.

Jacob broke the silence. "I have to head back to the North Camp with Tabitha in a few minutes. I would love it if you would join us. It would give us some more time together. I have some things I want to show you there."

"I don't think I'm ready for that, Jacob. I'm sure my mom is missing me quite a bit by now. I may need to head back to Kansas and check on her and the farm."

"Gabriel, please . . . don't go. This is your home."

"With all due respect, I'm not sure home is supposed to feel like this."

Gabriel stood up and walked back toward his room.

Jacob left and found Tabitha. They said their goodbyes to the team and loaded their gear into the Jeep. Jacob sat in the driver's seat with the engine running while Tabitha paid one last visit to Gabriel. She pecked on the door and pushed it open.

"Gabriel . . . are you here?"

Gabriel was collecting his clothes from the dresser and stuffing them into a duffle bag.

"Are you coming with us?"

"No, I'm not."

"You're not leaving for good, are you?"

"I'm leaving. I don't know for how long."

She walked to him and took his hands.

"Please don't go. We need more time . . . more time together."

"I just can't stay. I've gotta work this out."

"Work it out with me!" she begged.

"I don't think that'll work."

"Will you come back soon?"

Gabriel looked her in the eye without expression.

"I don't know."

"Then goodbye, Gabriel." Tabitha's eyes filled with tears as she blew him a kiss.

"Goodbye."

CHAPTER 23

A Trip Home

Gabriel took a break from packing his things in the dingy cabin room and sat on the edge of his single bed, alone—very alone—with his thoughts.

His summer at The River had started with such hope and promise. He was discovering a vision of whom he could become, his purpose in life. He was starting to belong and find his way. Experiencing the beauty of The River, the camaraderie of new friends, the mentorship of Jacob, and the love of Tabitha couldn't be topped. All that, however, was now shrouded in a dense fog of hurt, grief, and unforgiveness.

He didn't know what to do next. He didn't want to go back to Kansas, but it was too hard to stay. He felt like the walls to his soul were closing in. While methodically packing his belongings and fretting about what to do next, a thin shaft of light came through a crack in the closed draperies—the only light illuminating the room. In the shadowy space, he could feel the sadness moving in on him, much like when he was a child.

Back in elementary school, his "hard days" would grab his emotions and suck him down like quicksand. Terrifying thoughts wouldn't let go until they had pulled him under. Out of the corner of his eye, he noticed The Journal sitting on his nightstand. He picked up the volume and thumbed through it, thinking maybe something there would bring guidance and clarity to his troubled soul. A certain page caught his attention, so he started to read an entry from his father, John Clarke:

Today was ridiculous and stupid. I just don't get Maggie at all. I'm tired of dealing with customers who are rude and don't respect The River. Some days I just want to quit. Life shouldn't be this hard . . . or should it? Where did I get the notion that my life should be any different than others? I don't know. I guess my old man was right. An easy life is overrated and boring.

So, what am I trying to say?

Don't make any big decisions on a bad day.

Gabriel closed The Journal and contemplated the timeliness of his father's entry. He was making a big decision on what had been a very, very bad day.

After a few minutes, he exited the room to the deck and took his place in one of the rocking chairs facing The River. Nothing had changed since Tabitha left: the afternoon was still lit by a sun-filled blue sky, the fast-moving water shimmered as it flowed, and a warm breeze played with the trees like fingers through wind chimes.

Only a few minutes passed when the smell of pipe tobacco rolled in from one of the gentle gusts. A few moments later Ezra appeared, moseying up the stairs, pipe clenched in his teeth. Each hand carried a large tin cup.

"I brought somethin' for you. You like malts?"

"Sure." Gabriel's mood lightened.

"There's just somethin' about a chocolate malt on a warm summer afternoon." Ezra handed Gabriel one of the tin cups as he plopped down in the rocking chair next to Gabriel.

"Thank you." Gabriel immediately took a sip.

"You're welcome, my friend." Ezra smacked his lips after he swallowed his first sip. "Ahhhhhh," he sighed. "Mmmm, that's good."

"It sure is. What did you put in here? You always have some secret ingredient going on."

"A little chocolate, some malt powder, ice cream, and milk . . . and somethin' I can't tell ya."

They both had a good laugh as they enjoyed their chocolate treat and the picturesque view from the deck. Instead of more small talk, however, Ezra asked a direct question that caught him off-guard.

"So you gonna go up to North Camp to see Jacob and Tabitha?"

Gabriel wondered how he knew. "I found out some things today, Ezra . . . some things about Jacob—and Tabitha. I'm just not sure what to make of it all."

"I know. But I think you should go, son."

"I want to get past all this, I really do, but all I can think about is . . . he's the guy! He's the one I've been angry at all these years. I spent all that time with him and he didn't tell me."

Ezra paused for a few seconds. "I can only imagine what must be going through your head right now."

Gabriel said nothing. Ezra wouldn't get him to talk.

"You see that big rock out there?" Ezra pointed to a large moss-covered boulder in the middle of The River.

Gabriel nodded.

"I woke up one morning a few years back and that rock just showed up. Must have fallen from the mountainside in the night. It's funny how over time that rock has turned into a beautiful addition to the scenery here. That's because The River never stopped moving . . . in fact, over time the waters turned that rock into its own work of art . . . smoothing the rough edges, flowing around and over it. It's almost as if The River is showing off that rock like a trophy or something."

Ezra paused a moment, then resumed speaking. "Seems a little like life to me. The rocks fall, and we can't stop 'em or see em' comin'. We keep flowing . . . moving . . . living . . . and somehow, those experiences become the things that create the beautiful landscape of life. It's all in how you look at it."

Gabriel took another sip of his malt. "How is it that you see life that way, Ezra?"

"Time. I've got more time under my belt. I'm old, son."

The two chuckled at his response. Ezra shifted the conversation back to the heart of the matter.

"He cares for you a great deal, Gabriel. If he could take it back a thousand times, he would. But you know what?"

"What?"

"If it hadn't been Jacob, it would have been someone else. My guess is your father didn't know he wouldn't come back up out of that water. He just knew that if he didn't go in, a man would die. That's who your dad was. You see, this isn't about Jacob, young man. Your father did not lose his life because of Jacob . . . he *gave* it. There's a big difference. What drew you to Jacob in the first place was the man that he *is, not* the man he was. And Tabitha? Boy, you better not let her go . . . why she's the canyon princess!"

Gabriel relaxed. Ezra, as usual, was talking good sense.

"Maybe," Ezra continued, "instead of looking at Jacob as a reminder of what happened in the past, let him be a reminder of what a great man your father was. Jacob Fielding is living proof of your father's selfless sacrifice, and hey, if there had been no Jacob . . . there would be no Tabitha. We've gotta remember that The River brought us *all* together, and *that* is somethin' to be thankful for."

Ezra raised his malt cup to Gabriel for a toast. Gabriel smiled as they clanked their cups together.

"Ezra?"

"Yes-suh?"

"Thank you. I've got a lot to work through."

"One step at a time, son."

Ezra tipped his hat as he stood to leave. "Well, I better get back to work." The old sage hiked up his trousers and started down the steps. When he got to the bottom, he turned back over his shoulder.

"Oh, Gabriel. When you get back, let's play that game of marbles we've been talking about. I promise I'll take it easy on ya." Ezra flashed his contagious smile.

"You're on, my friend. You're on."

Gabriel didn't waste any time.

It didn't take him long to finish packing his things. He knew what he had to do. He loaded his duffel bags into his truck and then made his way to the kitchen, where he poked his head in the screen door. He found Ezra slicing vegetables on a large butcher block.

"I'll catch you later, Ezra. I'm heading to North Camp."

"That sounds good, young man. That over there is for you."

Ezra pointed to a brown paper sack on the counter. Gabriel opened the sack and found a folded piece of paper with some handwriting and a turkey sandwich wrapped in butcher paper. A can of crème soda was in the bottom of the bag.

"Thanks, Ezra! You know how much I love your sandwiches."

"Lettuce, pickles, and light mayo, right?"

"Perfect."

"Oh, and don't lose that paper. It's got the directions to North Camp on it."

"You're the best, Ezra!"

"I know, I know. Now get outta here."

Ezra beamed as Gabriel waved goodbye. With a spring in his step and a lunch sack in his hand, he hurried out the door. As his truck rumbled down the gravel drive and out onto the road, Gabriel was beginning to feel the crushing emotional burden he had carried all these years lighten. His journey to freedom had begun. He wasn't sure what was next, but he was willing to start the journey. He couldn't get to North Camp soon enough.

Two hours of winding through the breathtaking canyon roads gave Gabriel time to reflect on his journey thus far. With his windows rolled down, the mountain air gusting in, he daydreamed about everything that had transpired since the day he got the call from Jimmy. The road trip with Cig, Rollie,

and the gang; camping at The Beach; hearing The River speak to him in his dreams; the first time he locked eyes with Tabitha; and the first time he rode the big water. From a frightened little boy in Cairo, Kansas, who was scared of his own shadow, to a young man brimming with the promise of love and adventure, Gabriel Clarke knew he was coming alive.

His heart fluttered as he got close to North Camp. He picked up the scribbled directions from the frayed bench seat and took one more glance.

At the main intersection (there's only one) of CF, take a left and follow the signs.

Gabriel looked up at the road ahead and spotted a small sign glimmering in the late afternoon sun.

Welcome to Corley Falls
Population 768

His heart leaped. He hadn't been back to Corley Falls since he moved to Kansas sixteen years earlier. He still remembered the main drag. The two-pump gas station on the right, a bank branch, a couple of small diners—it all felt strangely familiar.

Gabriel slowed down when he passed what he thought was his old home. The two-bedroom bungalow looked so tiny! He made a left at the only stop sign in the center of town, then drove a few hundred yards and saw the large painted sign on the right side of the one-lane road:

John's Big Water Adventures
The North Camp

His father's namesake on the sign nearly brought Gabriel to tears. He made the right turn into the property and coasted down a steady incline to the gravel parking area. Dozens of rafters, finishing their day on The River, were getting into their cars and heading out as he entered.

Gabriel parked as quickly as he could and walked toward a rustic building where the wooden sign out front said "Main Office." He opened the screen door and was taken by the scene. Pictures, newspaper clippings, and memorabilia lined the walls of waiting area. As he got a closer look, much of what he saw were pictures of his father and grandfather. Faded articles from the "Grand Opening" in 1946, pictures of the first rafters to run with Big Water, and dozens of customer pictures—many with a beaming John Clarke—filled the office's left wall. Their transforming smiles told the story of their life-changing experiences on The River.

"Gabriel!"

Tabitha came running around the counter and jumped into his arms, pressing her face into his shoulder. To Gabriel, it felt like she was hanging on for dear life.

"I'm so glad you're here!" she exclaimed.

"Me too. Me too." He squeezed her again.

"Hey . . . ."

Gabriel set her down in front of him and grabbed her shoulders. "I'm really sorry for the way I acted."

"It's okay."

"No . . . it's not. I was a jerk. It just happened so fast. Your dad and everything . . . I don't know how it's all supposed to go

right now. I have to work through some things, but I know that I can't leave just yet. I really want to be here . . . with you."

Tabitha hugged him again. "You know I feel the same way about you."

Relief cascaded through Gabriel's shoulders. Tabitha had accepted him in his best and his worst moments. She was gold.

"Aren't these pictures amazing? Look at this one over here." Tabitha pulled him over to the wall and pointed to a faded newspaper clipping. Gabriel moved in closer and squinted to see the smaller picture. There was John Clarke, standing in front of lodge with his hand on the head of a blonde four-year-old boy.

"That's me!"

"You see that look on your face? Growing up, I always wanted to meet that boy. You know why? Because I saw adventure in those eyes . . . and he was really cute."

"I think I remember that day. I recall Dad saying something about smiling for the paper and that I was going to be famous."

Tabitha took both his hands into hers. "Gabriel, this was your family's camp. My dad bought it after he found out the rafting operation was in foreclosure. He kept the name 'John's Big Water Adventures' as a tribute to your father's legacy."

"I'm blown away. I don't know what to say. When I saw the sign out front, the hair on my neck stood up."

"That's why I wanted you so much to come up to North Camp. You had to see this for yourself."

"You were right. It's amazing."

An awkward pause ensued.

"You haven't seen the operation yet, have you?" Tabitha asked.

"Nope, I've been here only a few minutes."

"Great. I wanna show you around."

"I would like that."

They walked behind the counter and out the back door. When Gabriel and Tabitha reached the bottom of the four wooden steps, they looked up—and there was Jacob, standing a few yards away.

Tabitha's father stopped dead in his tracks, and then a slight and wondering smile emerged on his face.

"I'm so glad you came," Jacob said tenderly.

"Thanks."

"I can only imagine how difficult this was for you, son."

Gabriel's demeanor softened even more at Jacob's choice of words.

"Ezra helped me to see some things . . . ."

"Ezra's a wise man. I've been listening to him since I was a little shaver. Gabriel . . . I'm so sorry. I hope that someday you can forgive me. I'm not sure where we go from here but . . . well, I'm just really glad you came."

He stepped closer to Gabriel. His steely blue eyes reddened with sorrow.

A few seconds of silence ticked by.

Gabriel lifted his head. "I'm not sure either . . . about where we go from here. I have a lot of questions, ya know? I'm ready, though. I want to—"

Gabriel's countenance crumbled, and he buried his head in tears. Tabitha leaned in and held him.

After gathering himself, he looked to Jacob, who was wiping away moisture around his eyes as well.

"Sounds really good to me," Jacob said.

No more words were spoken in that moment, but none were needed. Their connection was real and palpable.

Jacob motioned for Gabriel to follow him. "I've been waiting to show you something."

Tabitha excused herself. "Someone needs to cover the office. I'll catch up with you guys later." Tabitha patted Gabriel and headed back to the main building.

Jacob placed his hand on Gabriel's shoulder and squeezed as they walked. "The North Camp at Corley Falls is a special place, Gabriel. Since I bought it many years ago, I've done a lot of work to the place, lots of upgrades and such, but there's one place I haven't fixed up much. I figured maybe you'd have some ideas of what to do with it."

Gabriel wondered what he meant.

The two men walked down a rough path that took them to the backside of the lodge that faced The River. A room, appearing to be an add-on, jutted out from the back with windows on three sides. Jacob stepped up and opened the door for Gabriel, who walked in first. Jacob followed and quickly opened the blinds to let the light in.

Gabriel's mouth dropped open with a sense of awe.

"This is . . ."

"Yeah . . . your father's old office."

Austere and sparse, the few items that lay around the old room were priceless treasures. A rustic wooden desk with a solid wood bankers chair faced the window toward The River. A few pens in a cup, a rotary dial telephone, and a large mason jar of marbles sat on the desk. To the left, hanging on a hook was an old, faded orange life vest, a paddle, and a marred white helmet with the hand-painted name "C L A R K E" across the back.

On the floor, he saw a pair of old hiking boots, dirty and weathered. One wall contained a small chalkboard with a few illegible markings. A solitary sepia-toned picture was pinned to a small bulletin board on the other side of the room. The old photo showed John standing knee deep in The River just outside the lodge, holding his young son. Gabriel sat down in the desk chair and rested his forearms on the desk.

After several moments of silence, Jacob spoke up. "All these things were in here when I bought the place. I like to come in here when I just need to think."

Gabriel ran his hands over the desktop. He felt the gauges and nicks from years of use. His eyes were drawn to what he felt with his left hand, the letters "M A G G I E" carved diagonally in the bottom left corner. He tried desperately to maintain his composure.

Gabriel felt so connected to his father in this moment. He imagined his father sitting there, talking to him . . . planning their next trip. He saw sketchy memories of himself coming in that office, begging his dad to play marbles or take him camping.

Jacob walked over to the window and pulled the blinds all the way up. A perfect view of The River was revealed. He turned and looked at Gabriel.

"It's yours if you want it."

Gabriel looked at him with a puzzled brow and hidden smile.

"This office. It's yours. I want you to come stay here, Gabriel. I need a lot of help around camp, and you're just the man for the job. I have a cabin for you, all your expenses paid, and a nice salary. Corley Falls is your home. In due time, you could be running the place. Having a Clarke at the helm of North Camp would feel right. But for now, come and work with us. I'll personally train you and show you everything I know. You will be a great guide . . . the best . . . just like your father.

"What do you say?"

Gabriel's eyes pooled with joyful tears. Biting his lip, trying desperately to remain in control and choke back his emotion, he kept nodding his head. He pushed the chair back, stood to his feet, and lunged into Jacob's arms.

"You got a deal."

"That's wonderful to hear, young man."

"I'm home, Jacob. I was *made* for The River."

EPILOGUE
FROM THE AUTHOR

"Ladies and gentlemen, we are about to begin the boarding process for Flight 723, service to Nashville. We certainly thank you for your patience."

That's all I heard of the distorted intercom announcement from the gate agent directly across the concourse.

"That's me," I said to Gabriel.

"Great to meet *you*, my friend." The rugged fifty-something adventurer extended his arm.

His calloused hand met mine. "Great to meet you. And thank you for sharing your story."

We broke from our handshake, and he looked at me intensely. "It's important to do that, ya know . . . share your story. Remember . . . everyone has a story."

"I wish I had time for more." I slung my backpack over my shoulder.

"I'll make you a deal. Look me up and come run The River with me sometime. I'm talking the big water. You do that . . . and I'll fill you in on the rest." The outdoorsman flashed an audacious grin.

"You've got yourself a deal!"

I waved goodbye and headed to the gate and down the jetway.

The hours that passed seemed like minutes. I was excited to head home, but my soul wanted to hear more. Gabriel's story of how he bade farewell to Cairo, Kansas, that summer of 1971 and embarked on a path to become one with The River moved me to my core.

I took stock of my life that night on the flight home. I thought about the blessing of my wife and kids and how I never . . . ever wanted to take them for granted. I thought about how much time I spent worrying about climbing the corporate ladder, chasing the little things . . . power, money, notoriety.

Weary of comparing myself to other people and settling for the "flatlands" of life, I thought about how I, too, was made for more . . . I was made for "The River" as well. I thought about the people I needed to forgive . . . and the people I needed to ask to forgive me.

I uttered some prayers that night on Flight 723. Gabriel's journey reminded me that we are all part of a much larger story. His passion for The River was undeniable and contagious. I didn't want to sit on the banks any longer. I wanted to get in . . . all the way in. I wanted to ride the "big water" now.

You see, Gabriel actually did it—something that very few

are able to do. He joined the ranks of those who dare to leave the safety of what they've always known for a better place . . . a place they were destined for from the beginning. No longer obligated to the chains of fear, grief, and resentment, Gabriel took hold of not who he was, but who he was to become.

Forever captured by The River, he was a new man,

free to live with adventure,

to love with abandon,

and to be loved.

He would never be the same.

The world . . . would never be the same.

ACKNOWLEDGEMENTS

To say that it took a robust amount of help and encouragement to get me to the finish line with *The River* would be an extreme understatement.

To my wife, Leah: You walked through every step of this journey with me, making sacrifices and urging me to finish. You've lived with each and every character and scene as much as I have, and you've joined in every emotion along the way. You lifted me when I struggled and celebrated at every milestone. Listening, advising, and encouraging—without you, this dream would not have become a reality. My words fall short to describe my gratitude and love for you.

To my beautiful kids Micah, Maisie, and Wyatt: Thank you for supporting your dad and dreaming with me about all of the possibilities. You are the most creative and exciting kids I know. I love you all so very much.

I'm also grateful to all of my friends and colleagues who got in the raft and put a paddle in the water with me.

First and foremost to my editor, Mike Yorkey: Your wisdom and expertise, guiding me through this process, shepherding this new author, was a true godsend. You were gracious, patient, and always ready with an uplifting word. Whether shaping a scene, developing a character, or creating dialogue, you helped me stay true to my style and voice. This book became a reality because of your help. You make it look easy . . . and it's not! I'm eternally grateful.

To Bob and Bonnie Neale, my mom and dad: Thank you for all your support and encouragement . . . for being amazing grandparents to our little ones . . . for always being there. I love you both.

To Mom and Pop Evans: Your love and support means the world. Thank you for all the wonderful holiday meals and memories and the way you cherish our kids. You are loved.

To Kurt Beasley: I'm so grateful our paths crossed many years ago. Thank you for walking this road with me with wisdom and discernment. Your insights and steady guidance have helped me stay the course.

To Steve and Julie Helm: Thanks, Steve, for pushing me out there to do it. You are a true brother. And Julie, thanks for being another set of "eyes" on the project. You guys are like family. We love you.

To the best of friends, David and Amber Loveland: The meals, the laughs, the rides to the airport, the futon, the parties . . . you guys are the best . . . sharing life with you is a joy beyond words.

To John and Holly Boswell: This project would not be possible without you. Thank you for your gracious hospitality, always ready with a room and a ride. You are generous beyond words.

To Dr. Todd Mullins, Dr. Tom Mullins, and Dr. John C. Maxwell: To think that I can call men like you my mentors is a gift beyond words. Thank you for your time and belief in me.

To Jordan and Nicki Rubin: Your message of good health and your mission to share that message has changed our lives. We are so grateful for your advice, encouragement, and friendship.

To David and Marla Saunders: Thank you so much for your generous hospitality. Your home was an oasis through such critical transitions. We are blessed to call you friends.

To Mike Smith: Thank you so much for your belief and encouragement. You are a treasured friend, and I love our coffees.

To Rick White: Thank you for giving me the opportunity to be creative and bring this story to its first venue.

To Bill Reeves: Thank you for helping me see the scope of what could be with this story. Your encouraging words have always been timely.

A big thank you to all of the owners of the "offices" I occupied during the writing process: The Good Cup, Meridee's, Puckett's in Leiper's Fork, Starbucks, the Boswell guest house, and last but not least, the only room left in all of metro Atlanta, Room 225 at the Econo Lodge just outside of Atlanta, where the last three chapters were written when I was snowed in for three days.

For More
on The River,
Please visit

THE RIVER EXPERIENCE.COM